Also by the same author

Child of the Hive
Shadows of Tomorrow

The Codename Omega series
Omega Rising

Jessica Meats

Codename Omega:
Traitor in the Tower

(Codename Omega #2)

Copyright © 2014 Jessica Meats.

All rights reserved. No part of this book may be reproduced, stored, or transmitted by any means—whether auditory, graphic, mechanical, or electronic—without written permission of both publisher and author, except in the case of brief excerpts used in critical articles and reviews. Unauthorized reproduction of any part of this work is illegal and is punishable by law.

ISBN: 978-1-4834-0841-5 (sc)
ISBN: 978-1-4834-0840-8 (e)

Because of the dynamic nature of the Internet, any web addresses or links contained in this book may have changed since publication and may no longer be valid. The views expressed in this work are solely those of the author and do not necessarily reflect the views of the publisher, and the publisher hereby disclaims any responsibility for them.

Any people depicted in stock imagery provided by Thinkstock are models, and such images are being used for illustrative purposes only.
Certain stock imagery © Thinkstock.

Lulu Publishing Services rev. date: 2/24/2014

Chapter 1

No one ever plans to become a traitor. I certainly didn't. I know there are several of the Guardians who use that word with great venom when they talk about me. I would like to remind them that my first act of treachery was on Nuke's behalf.

Nuke took me to one side in the dusty and cluttered warehouse that, back then, served as his base. It gave us an illusion of privacy, standing away from the others who were moving around the place, busily working. We stood behind one of the larger machines, an unknown mass of plastic and metal with cracked casing and an aerial attached with duct tape. In the gloom, Nuke's face was shadowed and serious. The worried lines that crossed his forehead made him look older.

"We need to know more about Grey's Tower," Nuke said.

I nodded. We were still very much in the dark about Grey's Tower and Mrs Grey's plans. Until we knew more, we didn't really stand a chance of stopping her. I felt the chill of dread as I knew what he was about to ask of me. I didn't voice the idea in the flimsy hope that I was wrong.

"We need you to go back into the Tower, Omega," Nuke said, confirming my fears. He used my codename, perhaps trying to remind me that I was one of them now. That I owed them. I felt very young, as though my existence had been stripped of all autonomy, despite the fact I was officially an adult. I could have said no. I wanted to, but I had nowhere else to go, short of running back to my parents like a frightened little girl.

Besides, I wanted answers about Grey's Tower as much as anyone and logically it made sense. I was still technically a Tower employee.

"Mrs Grey isn't likely to trust me now," I pointed out. We'd used my security pass to break into Grey's Tower. Even if no one had seen my face, the question would be there in everyone's mind.

"We just have to convince everyone that you weren't complicit in the attack on the Tower," Nuke said. "We have to make it look like we took your pass without your help."

I nodded.

Nuke hit me.

He slapped me round the face with enough force to knock my teeth together and leave me blinking and dazed. I stood in front of him, waiting, while Nuke brought his hand back to hit again.

"She wouldn't have just stood there," Knight said, coming over from where he'd been packing up equipment. He gestured to Nuke to get on with the clear-out effort. They were sacrificing their base to make this whole thing seem more real, which meant deciding what they could afford to lose and moving the rest to a safe location.

The only thing more important was making sure it looked like they'd taken my pass forcefully from me.

"Block," Knight said. Then he started punching.

He dealt a series of punches, straight and roundhouse in a repeating pattern. I stood in front of him, blocking again and again until my arms stung from the repeated contact. Knight didn't hold back. He also didn't look me in the eye, his gaze fixed on a point just above my face even as he attacked. Was he still angry that I hadn't told him I was involved in this mess? Because he hadn't told me either, so really it was unfair for him to blame me. Maybe he blamed me for the bruises that decorated his face? His swollen and split lip? For Victory's death? For everything?

I wanted to break down in tears, to tell him that I would never do anything to hurt him. Instead, I stood in silence and blocked over and over. My arms were blossoming red with fresh bruises, my muscles tired and sore. I mistimed a block and a punch grazed against my chin but Knight didn't slow. He didn't hesitate when another punch caught me in the stomach. Another punch caught my face again and I tasted blood against my lip.

Was it only a week ago that we'd sparred as friends in the university sports hall? Back then, I'd only known him as Ethan. He'd been so kind, so concerned with not hurting me. Now he punched as though he wanted to watch me bleed.

Tears stung my eyes. I let him think it was from the physical pain.

Knight was breathing hard, his dark hair damp with sweat, when he finally stopped punching. Those eyes, which had been bright with intelligence and laughter when I'd talked to him as Ethan, were now sharp and cold. He switched to kicks instead, dealing a few roundhouses to my thighs. One caught me right on the point of my leg where a recent burn was still healing. I gritted my teeth against the pain.

When he stepped away, I felt like a punch bag. My limbs ached with pain, my head throbbed in time to the beat of my heart. But Knight wasn't done. He grabbed a coil of rope from one of the counters and took me to a chair, tying my wrists and ankles tightly.

"Try to escape," he said. Then he turned and walked away. He went back to packing up, working under Navy's direction as they teleported away anything they couldn't afford to lose, disassembling some of the bigger equipment to fit it into the person-sized compartment in the teleporter. I wasn't sure where they were moving the kit to. Maybe Nuke thought it safer if I didn't know. Maybe he didn't trust me.

I sat in the chair, squirming against the ropes until my skin was scratched and raw, watching the others work. They were all busy, Nuke's little army. Nuke was extracting components of alien tech from the machinery that lay around the old warehouse they had used as a base. As well as the alien oddments, there had been a lot of ordinary computer components used and those could be safely abandoned. Princess and Valiant were packing into boxes whatever Nuke gave them. Knight now worked with them, boxing up weapons and my Omega armour. Navy was sorting through smaller pieces, sometimes adding them to the boxes, sometimes setting them aside with a sigh, to be lost to Mrs Grey. He was also working on the explosives.

The teleporter was the Guardians' greatest advantage. They weren't going to let Mrs Grey get hold of it, but neither could they teleport it away safely. So Navy was rigging it to blow up, once they'd stripped it of whatever parts they could get away with.

They carried box after box into the teleporter, taking them to some other place, but the warehouse still looked cluttered, full of scientific equipment, broken weapons and scraps of scavenged, half-repaired, mess. I didn't know what most of this stuff did. Now I wouldn't have the chance to learn.

When Nuke announced that they'd moved the most important pieces, it was time for phase two of the plan. He turned on one of the remaining pieces of equipment, a small black circle lit with glowing symbols that flowed across the dark surface. It was hauntingly beautiful. It was also alien technology which Mrs Grey should be able to track, particularly since Nuke had already removed half of the Guardians' shielding technology.

We couldn't know how long it would take for the Grey's Tower security forces to investigate. They didn't have the teleporter so it wouldn't be instant, but we couldn't be sure if they'd use vans or alien aircraft. We had to be ready for either.

The Guardians were already in their armour, but now they donned their helmets, hiding their faces away behind tinted visors. It was somewhat of a relief not to have to look Knight in the face, but now the real work began.

"What is the purpose of Grey's Tower?" asked Nuke. And so began the interrogation. I would protest that I didn't know; he would rephrase the question and ask it again. I would state that I'd only been working there for three weeks; Nuke would say he didn't believe I'd have led teams into battle with as little knowledge as I claimed to possess. It went on for what seemed like hours, with us going round in circles, questions failing to yield answers.

It wasn't difficult to act scared and in pain. The bruises from earlier were now beginning to throb and I was worried about what might happen if someone saw through this charade.

I'm not sure how long we kept at it: probably more than an hour. There was no sign of the Tower security teams approaching until they attacked.

There was a crash of breaking glass and a canister dropped to the floor, fired through one of the high windows. As it hit, it sprayed smoke. Nuke and the Guardians were somewhat protected by their helmets. I was trapped in the growing cloud, coughing and choking, my lungs crying out for clean air.

I can't remember that fight clearly. It was all chaos and confusion: smoke, light, and noise. Weapons fire cut the air, both normal bullets and the flash of the Guardians' energy guns. Things smashed somewhere in the smoke. I heard voices shouting over the fighting, but most of the words were lost over my own coughing. My eyes stung from the smoke, tears blurring what was already indistinct.

I was trapped in the middle of it all, people moving all around me, just shadows in the smoke. I tried to ask for help. Something caught my chair and I fell, landing heavily on my side. My arm was pinned between the chair edge and the floor, my weight pressing down on already bruised flesh, but at least the air was marginally clearer.

I heard Nuke yelling, calling a retreat to the Guardians.

Then came the now recognisable whir of the teleporter powering up and the associated lights. Someone else was yelling a warning that the targets were trying to escape.

The teleporter blew.

Fire burst out in a blinding instant, sending a rain of shrapnel across the warehouse. Something sharp hit my leg. More things struck my side and arm.

The explosion must have caught one of the wooden worktops or perhaps a volatile piece of alien tech, because the flames didn't die. Dark, angry smoke added to the chaos as the fire built.

Someone yelled an order to fall back.

I screamed for help between coughs, trying to force enough air into my lungs to produce a decent yell. Each breath was painful. I strained against the ropes, mentally cursing Nuke for leaving me to die for the sake of his plan.

Desperate tears were streaming down my face, not just from the smoke. All I could think was that I was going to die here, despite potential help all around me, because I couldn't make myself heard. My last memories of that night are of still fighting to scream even as I slipped away.

Chapter 2

I woke slowly. Painfully. Each breath was laced with agony: my throat raw, my chest aching. My head throbbed. My limbs were stiff and sore. Even my eyes, when I blinked them open, stung. It seemed that every part of me had been put through a wringer.

Thoughts were slow and sluggish. I blinked blearily at my white surroundings, trying to recognise where I was. I was in Grey's Tower, in one of the medical rooms on the upper floors. Everything around me was crisp and white, disinfectant-clean. Turning my head to look was about all the movement I felt capable of.

My breaths, slow and laboured, were fed by a mask over my mouth. I wondered about removing it but that would involve moving. So I just lay there, cataloguing my pains, breathing air from the mask into my tortured lungs.

Along with the physical sensations, I felt angry. I was furious with Nuke. I knew he'd intended for this to look plausible. He wanted to convince the Grey's Tower security forces that I really had been a prisoner, but I couldn't help feeling that he'd risked my life to prove it. He'd cared more about getting a spy inside the Tower than he had about me getting hurt. I'd seen him fight to save Ethan and Casey, but now I'd seen another side of him, a man who'd leave me in the smoke to see his plan succeed. Maybe I was being unfair on Nuke. After all, he hadn't known the Tower forces would use smoke bombs. He might not have realised that the explosives would set off a real fire. At the time though, I hated him. I only had the word of people like Ethan and Adam that he was one of the good guys, and that wasn't enough for me. I was as likely to put my faith in him as I was to trust Mrs Grey.

I wasn't left alone very long. I'd probably only been awake five minutes when a medic came to check on me. When I tried to speak, the words grated painfully against my throat.

She told me not to talk and I was all too happy to obey. She helped me move my mask and sit up so I could sip from a cup of water held in front of my mouth. The water helped a little to soothe the rough dryness of my throat, but the pain resumed almost at once when I stopped drinking. Unfortunately, now I had to deal with a breathless feeling as though I'd just run a mile. My body was craving air, trying to force more into my lungs, which started me coughing.

The medic helped get the mask back over my face and I sucked in the oxygen between coughs, as the fit subsided.

My eyes were streaming when I finally got my breathing under control, partly from the coughing but partly from pain. The coughs had made my body jerk and made me aware of just how much every part of me hurt. I mentally cursed Nuke as I flopped back on the pillows.

The medic told me I was lucky, though I felt far from it. Apparently there wouldn't be any permanent scarring on my lungs.

A few minutes later, Lucy came to see me. Lucy was Mrs Grey's assistant, a fierce woman who ruled the Tower with a watchful eye. She took a seat at my bedside and asked me how I was feeling. Before I could answer, the medic insisted that I shouldn't be strained or forced to talk. So Lucy found me a notepad and pen.

I was grateful that medical orders would protect me from a real interrogation. I took the writing implements and then there followed the strangest conversation I'd ever had, with me trying to write answers to Lucy's questions as simply as possible.

"What happened?" Lucy asked.

I scribbled an answer: *They found out I worked for Tower. Thought I'd set up Ethan. Wanted to know about Tower.*

"Did you tell them anything about Grey's Tower?"

Don't know anything.

I wasn't sure if a piece of paper could convey an aggrieved tone, but Lucy seemed to understand. I'd been left in the dark, by the Tower and by Nuke.

"Do you know how they got into the Tower?"

Stole my pass.

Lucy nodded, "We thought you were working with them."

I turned sharply, a look of fake surprise quickly vanishing under a very genuine wince of pain.

The strange interrogation continued a little longer, with questions about Nuke's warehouse, what I'd seen there, what I'd heard. I gave short, simple, and almost useless answers. I learned more than I gave; apparently the lab had been almost completely destroyed in the fire. They'd not managed to learn anything about Nuke's origins or who his team was.

"Did you discover any names?"

Codenames. Nuke, Navy, Knight, Princess, Valiant, Omega.

I included my own codename in the list. For a moment, I considered making up a few more so that Nuke's team seemed more of a threat, but I decided it was a mistake to try and elaborate. I simply stuck to answering the questions I was asked.

"Did you see much of Omega?" Lucy asked.

I shook my head, scribbling again. *Saw him briefly. Others called him in. He vanished as soon as all came back.*

The interrogation didn't continue very much longer, but Lucy still had some bombshells to drop. She questioned me a little further about what I'd seen and heard before she asked the big question.

"Did you talk to Ethan?"

The memory of the conversation flooded back, the way he'd looked when he'd said he needed time, the way he'd refused to meet my eyes and then jumped at the chance to cause my bruises. The tears that filled my eyes were entirely genuine and I didn't try to fight them. For once in my life, I let my vulnerability show. Salty tears flowed down my face to the pillow, damping my hair on the way. Sobs shook my body as violently as the earlier coughing and my hands shook as I tried to write.

He hit me.

***

It was a fine line. I wanted to appear hurt enough that they believed the Guardians really had treated me as an enemy, but strong enough that Mrs Grey would want me on the team.

I didn't cry publicly again, but I let the pain out when I was alone, knowing that the cameras were probably catching every moment of it. It was surprisingly easy to bring the tears to the surface. All I had to do was think about Ethan walking away, then leaving me in the smoke as though he didn't care.

I'd never felt more alone than I did then. I was stuck in bed in the middle of enemy territory, as much a prisoner as if they'd locked me in a cell. I couldn't trust those around me; every minute I had to think about how my behaviour would be interpreted. Then there was the physical torment. The bruises faded to dull aches, but the pain in my throat and lungs persisted. For the first day or so, just getting to the toilets was a chore, simple activities leaving me breathless. Even when I was dosed up on painkillers, coughing took over as soon as I left the bed.

Then there was the boredom and the constant, bitter cycles of my thoughts.

I had to deal with more questions during those days. Lucy came back a couple of times, treating me with politeness as she asked me to expand on what I'd scribbled last time. Then there were a couple of guys from the security team, who were a bit less hostile to me now. Maybe hauling me out of a burning building convinced them I wasn't trying to usurp their positions. Maybe they didn't think I was a threat anymore. Maybe they just pitied me.

I'd seen them around the security offices, but this was the first time I'd really spoken to them, though I was still doing very little actual speaking. They introduced themselves as Matt and Thomas, saying the names as though the two of them came as a pair. They'd apparently both been in the team that had pulled me from the warehouse.

"Thanks," I croaked.

They asked me the same sort of questions Lucy had, as well as showing me photos taken from the security cameras on the night of the attack on the Tower. I got my first clear view of what I looked like in the Omega armour. The figure in the photographs looked intimidating, larger and more powerful than I alone could ever hope to be. The grey Omega symbol stood out on the black chest. Looking at the pictures, it was impossible to tell that I was female.

"Did you see this person?" Matt asked.

I shrugged. "Briefly."

"Did you get any impression of how he worked with the others?"

I shrugged again. "They called him to help. He left after. I'd guess ally, but not one of them."

They obviously knew that there was something that set Omega apart. The differences in the armour were noticeable enough. Thomas handed me a few more photos. Me beating Dr Thorn. The reminder of such a horrific loss of control set a sick feeling into my stomach.

"He OK?" I asked.

"He'll be fine," Thomas said. I breathed again.

There was someone else I needed to ask about, simply to avoid any chance I'd blow my cover later by saying something I couldn't have known. I just wasn't sure how to phrase it in a way that wouldn't also give away my knowledge. I waited, mulling the potential questions in my mind as we wrapped up our interview. It was as Matt and Thomas were leaving that I spoke.

"I'm surprised Professor Swinson hasn't been to visit," I said.

Thomas froze in the doorway. Matt nearly dropped the photos.

"You didn't know?" asked Matt. "He's dead."

I must have done a good impression of shock and distress. I wasn't surprised: I'd found his body. But the grief was genuine. I only had to think about him in his lab, excited about his experiments, or teasing me about my behaviour over Ethan, and pain bubbled up to the surface again. I forced back tears, my fists clutching at the blankets on my bed.

"How?" I asked.

"I'm not sure," Matt answered. "He was killed in the attack."

"Photos?"

Matt skimmed through the pile in his hands, "Not of that. Sorry."

Of course they wouldn't have photos of that, because Swinson hadn't been killed by the Guardians. Mrs Grey was playing games with her own security teams, mixing truth with lies and giving just enough information to convince them that the Guardians were brutal monsters.

Matt came back to the bed, placing a hand on my shoulder in an awkward attempt at comfort.

"We'll get revenge," he promised.

I nodded, aware that I was just adding another layer to the lies. The hand against my shoulder felt cold and hollow, the gesture empty of anything that might have soothed my troubled mind.

***

I was bored senseless by the time Lucy came back to me, bearing a printout of another weekly payslip and a paper-clipped pile of paper. A faint sense of amusement made it through even my dismal mood at the thought that they'd be paying me for the past week. All I'd done was lie in a bed in their offices, eating their food, swallowing their painkillers and breathing their canned oxygen. The various interrogation sessions barely added up to a single workday.

Lucy also carried a plastic bag containing clean clothes. Given that I'd been in hospital robes for the better part of a week, those clothes seemed like manna from heaven. They also implied the promise of freedom. My breathing was clearer now; I wasn't using the oxygen mask anymore. I was feeling more than ready to get back out into the world.

She left the clothes bag at the end of the bed and took the seat beside me.

"We have to talk about what happens now," Lucy said. "Your initial contract has come to an end. I fully understand if you have no interest in renewing it."

She placed the paperwork on the sheets beside me. The visible page looked like the opening on the contract I'd signed a month ago. This time, there was no stated end date. This was why I was here. This was why I'd gone through all this pain. All I had to do was reach over and sign it and I'd have the inside position that Nuke had been so desperate for that he'd nearly got me killed.

"I want to get them back," I said. "I want to stop them."

Lucy wasn't to know that all the anger in my voice was directed at her and Mrs Grey for the murder of Professor Swinson. Let her think I hated Nuke that much. It wasn't so far from the truth.

She offered me a pen.

I flicked through the paperwork of the contract, seeing the phrases I recognised from the first time round. The pen hovered above the dotted line. Then I hesitated.

"No," I said.

"No?" Lucy's surprise was obvious.

"Not this contract. I'm not going to be left in the dark anymore. When I signed up, you didn't tell me that there was alien technology involved and that nearly got me killed. When they were questioning me, I realised how little I knew. If you let me in, if you tell me the truth, I will help you hunt those bastards down to the ends of the Earth. But if you expect me to just play the pawn in your games, then I'm out. Full disclosure, or I walk."

It was the longest speech I'd made since the fire and my throat felt like it was burning again. It was hard to keep an expression of calm determination when all I could think was that I really wanted a cough sweet.

A part of me wanted Lucy to just throw me out there and then. I could tell Nuke I failed and then try to remember what it was like to be normal, before I saw people I cared about being beaten and killed. Before I became a killer.

Instead, she just thought for a long while before nodding, "Alright.

I can't promise full disclosure, but we will share everything we can with you."

I was in. I had achieved the first stage of my mission and won their trust enough to get back inside the Tower. I signed the contract.

"Go home for now," Lucy said, "and try to relax over the weekend. I'll see you next week and we'll talk."

So I got dressed in the clothes she'd given me, which were more expensive than anything I'd have bought for myself, including a sleek new coat. I headed home, with my copy of the contract in my pocket and a sense of loneliness I couldn't quell. I should be feeling a sense of victory. I should be feeling something. But all that filled me was a numbness of grief, and the fear that isolated me more and more from those around me.

Chapter 3

When I finally emerged into the city after those days trapped inside Grey's Tower, it was as though the world had been transformed into the holiday season. Lights hung across the main shopping streets in the town centre, shops were displaying trees in their windows and snowmen and reindeer appeared as chocolates and ornaments everywhere. The square in the centre of town was in the process of being filled with wooden stalls for a Christmas market and a bright carousel spun children around on colourful horses while parents shivered beside it.

I walked through the city, the darkness lit by twinkling colours from all the decorations, and huddled inside my expensive new coat. I used to come to York to do Christmas shopping every year. When I was little, my parents would bring me and I'd go nuts for the toys inside the Christmas Angels store and try to get extra free samples from the fudge shop on Low Petergate. As a teenager, I'd wandered the streets with friends from school, moaning about teachers and parents alike as we hunted for things to buy as presents.

This had been my world and I'd been a part of it. Now I moved through the crowds like a ghost. All around me people were laughing and having fun, or just living their lives, making their way home through the cold. I wasn't one of them. I was a being of secrets and death.

I had nowhere to go and no one to talk to. I'd recently spent too much time sat inside a little room to just go back to my bedsit and wait around all evening. Wandering the city probably wasn't the best of plans either. I was supposed to be resting and I was starting to feel breathless despite it being just a slow walk. I was constantly aware of aching pains and the shortness of my breath.

I ended up alone in a restaurant. I was surrounded by business meetings, romantic dates, and friendly get-togethers. I sat there, moving food from my plate to my mouth in silence, feeling emptier with every bite.

***

I had no way to contact Nuke and let him know of my success. All I could do that weekend was try to pass the time. I read, I went to the cinema, I spent inordinate amounts of time walking through the city streets, battling with Christmas shoppers. I used some of my new cash surplus to get some more clothes suitable for the smart environment of Grey's Tower. I made some make-up purchases as well, for the first time in years. My bruises were mostly hidden beneath my coat, but there were some on my face, specifically a fading green and purple splodge on my cheek, that I was keen to conceal. I wasn't focused on any task. I was finding it harder and harder to be interested in anything. My mood trapped me alone with my thoughts, with the memories of all I'd seen and done inside the Tower. I just wished I had someone to talk to.

I got through the weekend and made myself into a facsimile of a smart businesswoman. Would other people see the emptiness in my eyes?

I was issued a new security pass on arrival, since my old one had been so severely compromised. I was also informed that Lucy had put a meeting with Mrs Grey in my diary for later in the week. Then I headed up to the security offices, surprised to receive a pleasant greeting. Thomas and Matt both welcomed me warmly. Some of the others showed less warmth but managed to hide the outright hostility that had been present before. I went to my desk and pulled up the official reports about the attack on the Tower and my supposed rescue from Nuke's forces. I wanted to see how it was viewed through their eyes.

The Tower security teams had two big priorities. One was obviously to make sure an incursion like last week's wouldn't happen again. That was being dealt with by some of the team who'd been here longest and who were intimately familiar with the security systems in a way I could never be. The second priority was the one I was supposed to be working on: tracking down the Guardians.

I had no idea where Nuke's new base was, so I was as blind as everyone else, but I was trying to muddy the waters rather than actually find anyone. Late in the morning, I pulled together a few key people to brainstorm the problem. I called in Matt and Thomas, of course, and Chris, who'd been the most civilised towards me when I'd first arrived. There were a couple of others who were field team leaders heavily involved in this business, so I couldn't easily leave them out, even if they were glowering at me for having the audacity to take charge of a meeting.

"I've had a lot of time recently," I said, "to think about the information we've got and I've had a couple of ideas I want to share. If you think I'm wrong, feel free to speak up."

"No problem," muttered one of the glowerers, a big guy called Jeremy.

"Why York?" I asked. "Of all the places in the world, given that they have technology that lets them teleport from one place to another virtually instantaneously, why would they have their base in York?"

There were nods from around the table. They'd been wondering the same thing.

"We've got three possibilities that I can see," I said. "One: it's a coincidence."

"Seems unlikely," said Chris. I nodded, to murmurs of agreement from around the room.

"Two: whatever reasons Mrs Grey had for choosing York as a site for Grey's Tower also apply to these guys. Or three: they came here because we're here."

More nods. They were all quick to agree that number three was the most likely explanation. I hadn't had a chance to talk to Nuke about his reasons for picking York, so I was also in favour of that answer.

"That's obvious," said Jeremy. "I don't see how it helps us now."

"The question is," I said, "Why? If they can teleport anywhere in the world, why would they need to be nearby?"

"Unless they can't," said Matt, as he leapt to exactly the conclusion I was hinting at. I gave him a grin.

"Exactly. What if their teleport thingy is short range? Or shortish? Maybe it takes loads more power to send people further or something."

The other glowerer, Damian, exchanged a snort with Jeremy, "Highly technical explanation there, sugar."

"She's talking sense," cut in Thomas. "If we restrict our search to areas within the radius we know they can teleport, probably closer to York than to the edges of that area, then we narrow our search considerably."

"Probably to the north of York," I added. There was confusion from most, but Matt was grinning.

"I get it," he said.

"What?" Jeremy asked, switching the focus of his glare.

"Since I've been here," I said, "almost every delivery, goods drop, exchange, or ambush site has been to the north of here. If the enemy are trying to pick somewhere to set up shop, it makes sense to go towards where we've historically worked."

"Don't tell me you're buying this?" Jeremy asked the rest of the room.

"Have you got a better theory?" asked Thomas. "It at least gives us somewhere to start rather than searching the entire planet."

Jeremy and Damian weren't going to be easily swayed. I had no authority to force them to follow my plan, but the other three were at least accepting of the idea. Matt had already pulled up a map on his laptop and was busy working out likely sites. A few minutes later, Matt and Thomas were side by side at one of their desks. I never did work out which of them actually was officially supposed to work where; they tended to encroach on each other's territory without asking. They were leaning over the computer, bickering and fighting for control of the mouse, even as they drew up plans of attack. Chris was more restrained whilst analysing what we knew of the warehouse to come up with likely characteristics of the place the Guardians would choose for their base.

Damian and Jeremy were determined to prove me wrong, working on their own ideas in isolation, but that didn't bother me because the others were quite optimistic that we now had a plan.

It felt nice that I'd been listened to and that I'd made a contribution that people appreciated and were acting upon. Shame it was a lie.

I felt more of a fraud than ever, sitting at my desk, pretending to be hunting down the Guardians. It was exhausting, constantly putting on a front. Even at lunchtime, when Matt and Thomas invited me to eat with them, I was having to play a part. They were cheerfully talking, stealing food from each other's plates and discussing ways to track the Guardians. I had to pretend to be involved, talking about how to find Nuke and the others, all the while thinking about how to lay red herrings.

I made it through the day and finally collapsed in my flat, sitting on the bed with a pile of takeaway, too exhausted to manage anything else.

***

Tuesday started much the same. I dragged myself out of bed and dressed in my disguise: my expensive suit and a make-up mask. It was a convincing costume of a dedicated Grey's Tower employee. I put on my determined smile and set off to the office. I was due to have my meeting with Mrs Grey, so I waited by the lifts for Lucy to escort me. Even with an appointment, my badge wouldn't let me up to the office. I guess they didn't completely trust me.

Walking into Mrs Grey's office took more courage than going into battle. I was acutely aware that she would determine the success or failure of my mission. My mind kept leaping back to the last conversation I'd had with Professor Swinson. He'd said I couldn't trust Mrs Grey, that what she was doing was dangerous. Then he'd died. What if she decided I was an enemy and killed me too?

Lucy let me into the big office on the top floor of the Tower. It was the same as last time, every expensive piece of furnishing perfectly in its place. Mrs Grey sat behind her desk, her pristine suit probably worth more money than I'd ever earned, her greying hair pinned into a precise bun. She gestured for me to take the seat across from her and then sat with her fingers steepled on her desk.

"Well, Miss Harding, you've certainly stirred things up during your time here."

"Um, thank you?"

Mrs Grey gave one of her faint smiles that came nowhere near her eyes.

"Lucy tells me that you want more information about our business here."

I nodded, "I nearly got killed when you sent me against Nuke's team without telling me that they were using alien technology. If you want me to work for you, I want to know whatever you know about the situation. What do you know about Nuke and his team? And the creepy Omega guy? What are they after? What might they have wanted the quantum thingamy for?"

I kept my questions on the subject of Nuke and the others, instead of asking the questions I really wanted to know the answers to. I couldn't just ask about Mrs Grey's real purpose without admitting how much I already knew, so I had to pretend that I bought her side of the story wholeheartedly. I just had to hope she'd buy my buying it and let slip something I could use.

Mrs Grey gave another of those smiles that wasn't really a smile and said, "You probably know more than we do, having spent time in their base. We have only your reports of your experience to go on."

"But you said they'd been attacking you for weeks. You must have some idea why."

"We can speculate. We believe the leader of this group is non-terrestrial, from the use of technology that he'd have no way to find on Earth. The best of our research hasn't managed to match the teleport abilities they've shown. Whether he is the vanguard of an alien invasion, or simply one man acting alone, is where we are forced to resort to guesswork."

I added Mrs Grey's comment to my own store of suspicions and speculations about Nuke.

"I can't believe it's an invasion," I said. "Half of their base was held together by duct tape and they use phones in their communications. I'd have thought an invasion, even an advanced guard, would be a bit less… I dunno… ad hoc."

"That is our conclusion as well," Mrs Grey said, "but it is little help in the effort of stopping them."

"You must know something else. You said this was a big, multinational effort to stop the aliens. Surely someone knows something about where Nuke comes from, how he can look human, what other technology he might have hidden away."

"Our work here is heavily classified and we are not privy to the secrets of the other branches, just as they do not automatically gain access to our research. I know that there have been incidents of alien contact and the aliens in question were human in physical appearance. Whether this is their natural shape or a disguise, we have yet to determine."

"Do we at least know how many might be hiding here on Earth?" I asked.

Mrs Grey leaned back in her chair, "That is a very good question."

***

There were lots of good questions but no answers. At least, no answers I would be able to obtain without arousing suspicion. I returned to the security desk and spent most of the day with Matt, Thomas and Chris trying to work out where Nuke's team might have moved to. At one point, Matt started pulling up CCTV feeds from central Leeds, which was still on our list as a potential site despite being slightly south of York. He was trying to get facial recognition software connected to the video feeds to hunt for Casey and Ethan, since there was enough footage of them to do a clear ID.

"I had no idea that these feeds were available to the public," I said, watching Matt work.

"They're not," said Thomas. He glared at Matt as he said it.

"We're hunting dangerous criminals with alien technology who've already proved they're willing to kill," said Matt. "Do we really want to get into a debate of morality verses legality?"

I didn't feel like arguing on that point, though a part of me wanted to correct him about Ethan, or at least ask the question of whether we were sure they were dangerous. I held my tongue. I seemed to be making headway in my mission of earning trust. I couldn't afford to blow it now by appearing sympathetic to my supposed enemy. So I watched Matt work and felt another layer of secrets added to the wall that surrounded me.

Chapter 4

I was heading home from work one evening, and had nearly arrived at my bedsit, when I was caught off guard by a cheerful voice calling my name. Megan came running up to me, bundled up against the weather. I wondered if something was wrong. Perhaps there was some danger that they needed to alert me about, but she was grinning.

"Jenny! Feels like I haven't seen you for ages."

She grabbed my hand enthusiastically and I felt something press into my palm. The crackling edges of paper. Megan's grin didn't waver as she pulled back her hand and left the note in my palm.

"How are you?" I asked, hoping she'd give me some indication of what this was about. She didn't. She gave an inane answer about being busy with uni essays.

"I can't stop to chat now," she said, "but we should do a girls' night. How about Saturday?"

I agreed, hoping that this was a plan and that I wasn't just condemning myself to an evening of overly cheerful chatter. She hadn't seemed this hyperactively chirpy on the occasions I'd met her before. When I'd met her in her Princess persona, she'd been serious and sensible. This bubbly alter ego might be more than I could take. She suggested a time and gave me her address. I made a point of getting my phone out to store the details she gave me and was able to take a peek at the piece of paper while I did so.

They are always watching you.

The note had to be referring to Mrs Grey's people. At least I assumed so, since Megan was unlikely to be warning me about Nuke spying on me.

I stopped myself from visibly reacting, scrunching up the note into my handbag as I returned my phone. We finalised arrangements for the girls' night, such as they were, and we went our separate ways. Shut up in my room, I fretted about the meaning of the note.

It was the word 'always' that bothered me. If Megan had simply warned that I was being watched, I'd have assumed someone was following me in the street or could access public CCTV footage as Matt had. 'Always' implied something more sinister. Was someone spying on me in my own home? While I slept? In the shower?

I wished I could get clarification, but all I could do was pretend that everything was normal while I went about my daily business. I counted the minutes until Saturday evening, when I hoped to finally get some answers.

I headed onto the university campus as dark was closing in, finding the accommodation block Megan had directed me to. She had a room in one of the newer blocks in Alcuin College, one of multiple, nearly identical clusters of bedrooms overlooking a little courtyard. Each group of rooms came with a kitchen. Megan's was bigger than my flat and would have been smart except for some unwashed crockery and a broken door dangling off one of the cupboards.

Megan was the same overly chirpy nightmare, hugging me far too enthusiastically as she let me into the kitchen. She made a show of offering me wine or tea and I chose tea; I was still on medication for my lungs and wasn't sure if it should be mixed with booze. She also pulled a Tupperware box out of one of the cupboards.

"Adam insisted we couldn't have a girls' night without these," Megan said, opening the box and offering it to me. It contained a batch of brownies, gooey with chocolate. My heart sank when I saw the brownies. I began to worry that this really would be an evening trapped with Megan, forced to socialise. My empty room had rarely seemed so appealing.

"I think he was jealous we didn't invite him," Megan went on.

"To a girls' night?"

Megan gave a shrug and took me through to her room, which was compact but neat. It was as I expected student accommodation to be, with a single bed and desk comprising most of the furniture. A teddy bear in a pink dress and tiara perched beside rows of psychology textbooks on the shelf. We sat together on the bed because there wasn't really anywhere else.

Now I got the first indication that something was going on. She mouthed, "Not yet," at me before proceeding to chatter inanely. We talked a bit about her course and how she was getting along. She went on at length about an experiment they were studying about people obeying orders to hurt others. I asked her whether she'd got a boyfriend. She said no. I quickly moved the conversation on because I had no intention of talking about Ethan. It was easier just to work my way through Adam's brownies and listen to her babble. Was she hoping that whoever was spying on me would fall asleep from boredom?

I got something useful out of that portion of the evening though. I asked Megan about make-up. I'd never really bothered with it before, but it seemed sensible to learn if I was going to keep getting bruises that I wanted to hide. She talked about foundation and concealer, what sort of colours she thought would work for me, and so on. I'm not sure how much sank in, but I was at least armed with something for the next time I needed to mask my wounds.

The conversations were exhausting. I was having to act cheerful and animated when all I wanted to do was ask what was really going on. It was easier to busy myself with brownies because licking chocolate ooze off my fingers meant that I could let Megan carry the bulk of the conversation. At last, Megan suggested we watch a movie. She got a disc out of a case and then hurried into the kitchen to microwave some popcorn. Three minutes later, she put the disc into her computer and positioned it so we could see it from the bed.

The production company logos had barely started when there was a flash of light and a strange tingling running throughout my body. This was teleportation. They'd obviously rebuilt the teleporter with the components they'd taken from the other base. I'd only experienced it a couple of times before and didn't like the feeling now any more than I had then, but I was immensely grateful that something was happening at last. The light faded and I was standing in a huge warehouse.

I looked around in surprise at my new surroundings, taking in what had changed. The building itself was different. This warehouse was a little larger, with a series of doors in one wall implying more rooms to this place. A lot of the equipment had been moved from the old base, but there was new stuff here. The mess remained the same. Bits and pieces lay on all flat surfaces, the alien machines crammed in wherever they fit without regard for order. There was still duct tape holding things together.

Standing among the machinery were Nuke and Navy. Navy activated the teleporter again and brought Princess to join us. She'd left all her bubbly act behind in her dorm room as though she'd switched Megan off to become Codename Princess.

"Welcome back, Omega," said Nuke. He greeted me with a nod and a fatherly smile.

"What's this all about?" I asked.

"You're being watched," said Navy, "and not via human technology. Someone is using sophisticated tech to eavesdrop on you wherever you are and watch you when you're in the open."

"All the time?" I asked.

"As far as we can tell." At least I didn't have to worry about them watching me in the shower. Navy started to explain how the technology worked but Nuke cut him off, saying that it was only important that I knew this was happening, not how.

"That's why we had to make the girls' night seem real," said Princess. "We don't think they know about me being involved with Nuke. As long as they think I'm just a friend of yours, we can keep in contact."

"So they'll think we're sitting in silence watching the film now."

"Not in silence." Navy was grinning, really pleased with himself. "I was able to get a few snippets of you talking and edit together syllables to get a few comments about the film inserted at the appropriate times, along with the crunching of popcorn of course. The disc Princess used has the additional audio built in."

I was both impressed and slightly freaked out about this. It also occurred to me how much effort had been put into finding me. So we got down to business. Nuke wanted to know what I'd learned from Mrs Grey.

"Not a lot so far, I'm trying to get her to trust me."

I explained about the work I was doing with the security team, including the plan to locate Nuke's new base. I told him where we were looking and our reasoning for that. Nuke grinned.

"Perfectly logical and perfectly wrong," he said. "Keep them chasing that wild goose for a while. It will give us time to recover."

I was glad that I wasn't going to lead Grey's Tower to Nuke by accident. I wanted to ask where they really were but decided against it. Nuke would tell me if he wanted to and I couldn't give something away by accident if I didn't know.

We talked about my meeting with Mrs Grey, ineffective though it had been. Nuke listened without comment to the news that the aliens could look human. Navy just nodded and said that they'd guessed as much.

We discussed how I was getting on with winning their trust.

"I think some of the guys in the security team trust me, but not all of them. It's hard to tell with Mrs Grey and Lucy. It probably helped that you left me to die in the fire."

Princess and Navy looked shocked. Nuke didn't, but he did have the decency to look ashamed.

"I didn't know it was going to get that bad so quickly," he said, "and once we'd started, it was better to simply continue with the plan. If we'd hesitated, it would have all been for nothing. I'm sorry."

Logically, everything he said made sense, but he hadn't been the one struggling with breathing difficulties for several days and dosing up on medication to hold pain and secondary infections at bay. I'd come close to death and he was willing to make excuses. Still, there was no point arguing about it now. I forced myself to ask the question that was terrifying me.

"How's Ethan?" I asked. Navy cleared his throat pointedly and I corrected myself. "Sorry. How's Knight?"

I'd accidentally violated one of the rules that preserved secrecy: always using codenames while in the base or in armour, never using them at any other time.

"Physically, he's fine," said Nuke.

"Emotionally," said Princess, "he's moping like an emo Twilight fan."

I managed a smile at that description for Knight, who could be so strong and confident. Inside, my feelings were as messy as the warehouse. I was shamefully delighted that he was feeling upset, because it meant that I wasn't alone in my misery. A part of me had secretly hoped he'd be here, ready to beg my forgiveness for ever doubting me and saying he wanted to get back together. The fact that he'd stayed away was both good and bad to my churning mental state. He was obviously too upset by the situation to face me but it also meant he wasn't about to demand a reconciliation.

"He's managing to continue his course," Nuke said. "We teleport him to his lectures and back again. We're relying on the fact that Mrs Grey probably doesn't want to make a scene in a busy university."

I nodded my agreement, "Secrecy is very important to her."

"How are you doing with the whole Knight situation?" Megan asked.

I shrugged the question away. I wasn't about to discuss my own desperate loneliness with people who were still near strangers to me. We might have been through battles together but we weren't really friends, no matter how we'd pretended for the sake of my hidden listeners.

It felt that we hadn't achieved much through this secret meeting, but I was immensely glad to not be quite so alone. There were people here I could talk to about Grey's Tower and alien technology and everything else. I felt the first spark of human connection in what felt like an age. It would be easier to continue acting normal knowing this.

We wrapped up our meeting, conscious of the time that had passed and the film duration, which was acting as our deadline. Nuke gave me a gift, a little silver pendant that appeared to be a simple ring of metal on a chain. There were matching earrings with smaller silver circles. They were smart enough that I could wear them with my business clothes but apparently if I placed one of the earring circles inside the necklace, it would send a signal to Nuke's forces.

"You can't use it to send a message," said Navy, "but it works as a distress call that we can lock onto with the teleporter."

Navy teleported myself and Princess back to Megan's university room, where the film was just finishing. We settled ourselves on the bed as though we'd been watching all along. I made my excuses and left as the end credits began to roll, but not before agreeing that we should meet up again next weekend.

As I left, Megan pulled me into another hug and gave me one last message, muttered into my ear so quietly I barely heard it.

"Good luck."

Chapter 5

Any comfort I might have got from the meeting with Nuke and the others had faded after another slow Sunday alone with my thoughts. I went into work on Monday still feeling isolated from the rest of the world.

The receptionist, whom I had finally discovered was called Helena, told me that Lucy wanted an update on our status. She'd arranged a meeting with me and other key members of the security team. The key members turned out to be Chris, which I was grateful for, and Jeremy, which I wasn't.

We gathered in one of the small meeting rooms on the floor above the security offices. I was finding it easier to navigate the labelling system of the meetings rooms. I still had no idea about the secret plans of Grey's Tower, but at least I could make my appointments on time. The four of us sat around an oval table and, before Lucy had even started to introduce the meeting, Jeremy leaped into explaining how I'd had absolutely no success with my notions of locating the base.

I felt like a small child being berated for not doing my homework properly. Every time I opened my mouth to explain the logic behind our actions, Jeremy cut me off to continue his rant. Eventually, Lucy raised a hand and Jeremy fell silent. She gave a quiet smile that had the weight of armies behind it.

"Perhaps we should let Jenny explain herself," Lucy suggested.

"Right. Yes. Erm…" Apparently being constantly interrupted had rendered me incapable of using the English language. I cleared my throat and started again, explaining that we'd felt locating the base was a sensible move and talking about our reasons for narrowing the search as we had. I nodded towards Chris, explaining that he had been analysing the characteristics of the building to try and find a similar site.

"We've been going by size mainly," said Chris, "but paying attention to location as well. The warehouse near York was in a relatively isolated site. We suspect that a new base would be similar."

"You suspect," muttered Jeremy. "All you've got is speculations and guesses."

"We're looking for a needle in a haystack," said Chris. "We need anything we can get to narrow the search. Once we've got a target, we'll look into the public records to see who's using the site, utility usage, and so on to see if we come up with any anomalies."

Jeremy scoffed, "You're tracking these people by seeing if they've paid their gas bill? That's no better a plan than guessing."

Lucy held up her hand for silence again before a full argument blew up across the table.

"They are guesses," Lucy said, "but logical ones. We cannot afford to rule anything out completely, but this gives a sensible starting point. Have you found anything?"

"Not really," I admitted. "But we've got a list of business parks and industrial regions that they might be using. We don't want to send in people to investigate and spook them into running again. Matt's trying to access CCTV footage so that we can observe the sites from here until we can narrow the search down."

Chris kicked me under the table when I mentioned Matt and the cameras. After the initial annoyance, I wondered if he might have been right. Should I have stayed quiet about Matt's investigation channels? He'd already admitted that it wasn't technically legal. Lucy either didn't notice or didn't care. Instead, she turned to Jeremy and asked him to explain the approach he was taking.

"We're tracking unusual signals," Jeremy said, "and energy emissions which don't match expected patterns. If they're using alien technology, they're bound to be giving off electromagnetic radiation."

"Unless they can shield it," I said. It felt good to be the one pointing out the flaws in the plan, particularly since I knew for a fact that the base was shielded.

"Then there's the teleporter," Jeremy ignored me. "We're working with Dr Thorn to expand the capabilities of his invention to detect the enemy's teleport activity. We're going to start in York in case they still have operatives in the area. Dr Thorn is confident that we'll be ready to go online before the end of the week."

Lucy nodded her approval. I found myself fidgeting with the necklace. I thought of Ethan, teleporting here to continue his university studies. Jeremy would be able to pick that up.

It was like someone had poured ice into my veins. I listened to Lucy wrapping up the meeting and sending us back to our work, but my thoughts were filled with fear. I barely heard a word. As we walked back to the security offices, all I could think of was that I somehow had to give a warning to Ethan.

Jeremy returned to Damian, announcing in a voice that carried across the office that Lucy approved of their plan and thought my plan was all guesswork. They were laughing with some of the other security guys. It took me a moment to recognise one of them, but I realised he was one of the men I'd kicked in the groin in my first interview. I guess he held a grudge.

"Smug git," Matt muttered. He and Thomas were waiting at their desk for us. Chris summed up the meeting for their benefit.

"Are you OK?" Thomas asked me.

I shrugged, "I just wanted to have something solid by now."

"These people know what they're doing," said Thomas. "They're used to hiding."

We went back to our search, but I couldn't get my mind off what Jeremy had said. I found myself fidgeting constantly with the necklace, wondering if I could use it somehow to warn Ethan. If Jeremy was right and they'd have Thorn's device working before the end of the week, I couldn't wait until my arranged meeting with Nuke.

I was staring blankly at a computer screen, failing to come up with a plan, when Matt said something. I started round to look at him, embarrassed to have been caught zoned out.

"You OK?" he asked. Everyone seemed to be asking me that lately.

I shrugged, "Just thinking. Trying to get the pieces to fit together."

"I know what you mean," said Matt. "There are so many things about this that don't make sense. I've been thinking about what you asked after the attack, about photographs. Why don't we have any security footage of them killing Swinson?"

At that point, I was torn. I knew that I was being spied on. The sensible thing to do was to try and dismiss Matt's concerns to convince Mrs Grey I truly was one of them. But I liked Matt. I didn't like lying to him and I certainly didn't like the idea of him working for people who I was reasonably sure were the bad guys.

So I hedged. I tried to think of an excuse to make it sound like I believed Mrs Grey's story, but made sure it was an excuse Matt wouldn't buy.

"Maybe there was something top secret in the lab that we're not allowed to know about," I suggested, "and they couldn't show us pictures without showing whatever it is that's classified."

"If that were the case, they could pixilate it or crop the photo. No. Mrs Grey is hiding something."

"She's paranoid about secrecy," I said, "but can you blame her? There'd be riots in the streets if this got out."

"Maybe," Matt said. He didn't sound convinced. Secretly I was glad; I wanted him to doubt Mrs Grey. I just couldn't admit my own doubts without blowing my cover. This double agent stuff was exhausting.

Fortunately, our conversation was interrupted by Thomas arriving to collect Matt and take him to lunch, with Chris and me tagging along.

When I finally got out of work, I walked home via the town centre and stopped by a stationery shop, where I purchased a new, leather-bound journal. It was a smart book that closed with a clasp, a little strip of leather holding the back cover to the front. The first thing I did when I got home was to start writing.

I couldn't just write a message to Nuke and the others. If people were spying on me there was too great a possibility that someone would read this. So I wrote it as though it really was a journal. I ranted for a bit about how annoying Jeremy was and how his plan was a stupid one because there was no way the enemy would still be hanging around York for their teleport signatures to be detected. Laced through my writing were the pieces of information that would tell Nuke that someone was planning on tracking them. When I'd finished, I wrote about my plan, in note form as though to myself. I hesitated but eventually wrote about Matt by dismissing his concerns. Hopefully Nuke would understand. Matt was a potential ally in this.

It was cathartic to write it all out, even if I had to think hard about the double meanings in everything. My messages had to be clear to Nuke without giving me away if someone else read the journal.

I closed the book, snapping shut the clasp. Then I took off my necklace, wrapped the chain around the book and looped it around the clasp. I couldn't be sure this would work, but that the teleporter could take things from behind solid walls, and it was the best way I could think of to ensure that Navy grabbed the book. I put the journal in my underwear drawer and took off my earrings. I put the circle of metal inside the necklace and the two clipped together as Nuke had said they would. Then I shut the drawer.

I turned away, hoping I wasn't imagining the line of light which appeared momentarily around the edge of the drawer.

I got on with my evening as best I could, trying to ignore my concerns. Had Navy teleported it? Had Nuke understood my message? Had I been compromised? Or were Nuke's guys reading my diary and deciding I'd truly joined forces with the enemy?

I desperately hoped that Ethan understood. I needed him to know that he was in danger. More than that, I needed him to know that I was trying to protect him.

I forced myself not to check the drawer all night. In the morning, when I opened it, the journal looked just as I'd left it. My heart sank for a moment but I looked inside anyway. Underneath my scrawl of writing was something new. Three dots and a line formed a little smiley face at the end of my entry.

Nuke had received my message. I could only assume he'd understood.

***

I went into work in a much better mood. For the first time in days, I felt like I was actually accomplishing something. If it weren't for me, Nuke wouldn't know about Jeremy's plan and Ethan would be in danger.

I was determined to show Mrs Grey some initiative as well, comfortable that this wasn't likely to endanger Nuke or anyone else. I arrived at work early to find Matt already at his computer. Thomas came in a few minutes later, gym bag slung over one arm and his hair damp from a recent shower. The office rapidly filled up so we didn't have long to wait for Chris to arrive.

"You're in a good mood," he said.

"That's because we're going to get results before those guys do," I said, glancing towards the other end of the office, where Jeremy and Damian were talking to one of the lab coats. I pulled up Chris's list of target sites, starting with an old industrial park near Leeds.

"We're going on a field trip," I said, "but first we need some toys."

I didn't really know anyone in the labs now that Professor Swinson was gone. I'd seen a few people while visiting him, but I didn't even know names. Fortunately, Thomas had been working at the Tower longer than I had. Security didn't tend to hang out with scientists, but there was a lab tech Thomas went to the gym with. While Thomas talked about his friend, Matt gave him a look.

"Should I be jealous?" Matt asked.

Thomas grinned, "You have to accept you're not the only guy I get hot and sweaty with."

Matt returned the grin, relaxing; then Thomas led me down to the labs.

The lab tech turned out to be a large guy called Steve with a walrus moustache that he justified as a charity thing. Thomas introduced me and explained I needed some help getting some equipment and wasn't sure who to talk to.

"Sure," Steve said. "I'll see what I can do. What do you need?"

"A remote control helicopter," I said, "or something along those lines. Something we can put a camera on so we can investigate sites without getting too close."

Steve nodded his understanding and directed us to Lab 7: aerodynamics and aviation.

"They've got an unmanned aircraft project," Steve said, "and might be able lend you a prototype."

I didn't have security access to go into Lab 7, but I knew my way around the intranet well enough to find the identities of the people who worked there and emailed them a request for a meeting, explaining what I wanted. A junior researcher from the lab gave me fifteen minutes and said that there was an older test vehicle that would be suitable, but she'd have to get it authorised. A few minutes later, I was explaining myself to Lucy.

She made me sign a new collection of forms to say that I was responsible for the device. I was the one who had to make sure that the device was never in unauthorised hands because, even though it was an older prototype, it was still classified technology. I was also the one held responsible if the device were to be lost or damaged. I had visions of my newly full bank account suddenly being emptied again if I dropped the thing. But I had what I'd asked for: an unmanned craft that we could use to investigate suspect locations.

Chapter 6

The guys weren't too happy about how little notice I'd given them. Matt, in particular, didn't seem keen on going out hunting for teams of armoured warriors.

"I'm not a field guy," he protested. "I'll stay here and work on narrowing down the list of target sites."

"We need someone to fly the drone," said Thomas. "And you've got leet joystick skills."

"Don't say 'leet'. You can't pull it off."

"But *you* can. Time to put all that Xbox practice to use."

Matt still wasn't happy, but Thomas stayed to persuade him while Chris and I went to arm ourselves. We took a couple of glue guns that Swinson had created to immobilise armoured enemies, which had the advantage that they didn't look like real guns. I wasn't keen on the idea of carrying weapons around a major city. I thought of my Omega armour and the energy gun that went with it, but there was no point wishing for that. It wasn't like we were expecting to have to fight anyone.

"You sure you're ready to be back in the fight?" Chris asked as we loaded up one of the black vans with the drone and its equipment.

"I need to be doing something useful," I said. It was nice to say something that was actually true. He nodded his understanding and got on with strapping crates securely into the corner of the van. The guns were rather less carefully concealed inside Thomas's gym bag, padded with a slightly damp towel.

Back up in the office, Matt was ready to go. He had his fully charged laptop loaded up with the likely target sites and a route to travel between them. By the time we got in the van, it was already growing dark, the winter night falling quickly. We made a short detour via my flat so I could change into jeans and more practical shoes; the guys had already stripped off their ties and suit jackets. I wondered briefly if the necklace would cause suspicion, but figured no one would notice once I had my coat and scarf on.

Chris took the wheel of the van, with Matt sitting shotgun with the target list and GPS. That left me and Thomas sitting in the back trying to pass the time with small talk. I asked about Matt. All the usual questions: how long they'd been together, how they'd met, stuff like that. In turn, Thomas asked me about my love life.

"The last guy I dated left me tied up in a burning warehouse," I said, "so it's not great."

"You really liked him?"

"Yeah. He was sweet, in a strong way."

I couldn't describe my feelings for Ethan and I wasn't inclined to. It was still too painful. Besides, trying to sum up that bubbling excitement I'd felt when preparing to meet him just seemed silly and girlish. I desperately wanted to seem like a professional. Then there was that worry constantly at the back of my mind that someone might be listening. I couldn't afford to seem too sympathetic towards Ethan and I couldn't bring myself to say anything worse than I already had.

"How do you think he was recruited?" Thomas asked.

I shrugged off the question and attempted to change the subject onto a safer topic. We talked about TV shows for the rest of the drive.

***

Our first target site was a new business park to the south of Leeds. Only a handful of buildings were officially occupied. It was time to see if the truth matched the paperwork. This location was low down our list in terms of likelihood, but conveniently located in terms of Matt's route.

We pulled into a parking space in front of a big building of steel and brick that had a banner along the front advertising flexible agreement terms for lettings. Some of the other car parks were occupied but there was a steady stream of vehicles heading for the exits as people finished up for the day.

The four of us unpacked the drone and its gear. The drone was about a foot and a half long, a craft of sleek metal that wasn't quite like a plane or a helicopter. A pair of wings was set with rotors on the ends that powered its flight and could be controlled independently. It was fitted with cameras at the front, rear, and underneath. There was an array of other sensors that we were completely ignoring for this mission. We just set up the screens which would display the camera feeds and vehicle status. There was a transmitter that would apparently work over a ten-mile radius, which was serious overkill for our mission.

Once everything was unpacked, Matt took out the controls. He positioned his thumbs over the twin joysticks that controlled the rotors. Slowly, and carefully, he powered it up. I held my breath, imagining having to explain what happened to Lucy if Matt crashed the thing into the roof of the van, but the drone rose slowly into the air an inch at a time. Chris opened the back doors and the drone drifted out into the night.

Outside, a thin rain was falling, reducing visibility. That had to be a good thing as it would make the grey drone difficult to spot in the grey air. It took Matt only a few moments to adjust to the effects of the rain on the craft and then he had the thing flying up to the first building. We watched its progress from the camera feeds. Matt flew it close enough to the window for us to see the empty office space within. It didn't take us long to be satisfied with the survey and then he moved on to the next.

We obtained a lot of footage of empty buildings and some of occupied offices where business people were going about ordinary work. I was relieved and disappointed at the same time. I was glad we hadn't traced Nuke, but a part of me had wanted something to happen.

"This was always a low likelihood site," Chris said as Matt guided the drone back. We didn't pack away properly. Thomas held the drone in his lap and I kept an eye on the rest of the gear as we drove to the next site.

The procedure was much the same as we checked out another couple of locations. By the time we reached the fourth site, it was well past normal business hours. As we parked up, a security guard came up to the van and asked what we were doing. I almost panicked, but Chris remained perfectly calm, saying that we were a start-up company looking for an office location. When pressed, he said that we imported high-end electronic toys from Japan and distributed them to the big stores. He even showed the drone as proof.

I don't know if the security guard believed him, but he let us go without complaint, advising us to make enquiries with the site's sales office if we wanted a tour of vacant lots. We decided to cut our losses on that one and move to the next site. It hadn't looked very likely and we didn't want to risk exposure.

In the end, we tried twenty different sites around Leeds, using the drone to spy on a huge selection of office buildings, warehouses, and manufacturing plants. None looked remotely like the location for a team of fighters equipped with alien technology. I supposed that was a good thing, but it was genuinely frustrating to know that I'd be going back to Jeremy's sneers.

We arrived back at the Tower in the early hours of Thursday morning, utterly exhausted. To my surprise, we were met by Lucy, who didn't seem to mind the fact that we were robbing her of sleep. After the initial confirmation that we hadn't found anything, she told us to take the morning to recover and then give her a full report in the afternoon. I went home for a few hours of fitful sleep and returned to the office at lunchtime, feeling just as wiped out as I had earlier.

Damian greeted me as I walked into the office. "I hear you struck out on your plan, love." He was grinning. A part of me wanted to slap that stupid grin off his face, but I remained civil.

"This was just the first attempt," I said. "There are plenty of other sites to try. How's your plan going?"

Damian's expression darkened and that told me all I needed to know. In our little corner of the office, Matt and I shared a look.

"We need to find something before they do," Matt said.

I wondered when this had become a competition. My momentary surge of camaraderie was instantly followed by a surge of guilt because I was working against the very people who were trying to help me.

***

The week ended as a no-score draw. Our search of Leeds had turned up nothing, but initial tests of Dr Thorn's amended device had proved inconclusive. I supposed that meant I could have my meeting with Nuke without worrying about being tracked. I spent Friday evening and Saturday morning working out what to say and trying to come up with a new way to be useful.

I went round to Megan's in the afternoon, bracing myself for the overly cheerful act. I put on the mask of a friend having fun as we chatted. In her room, Megan scribbled on a scrap of paper without ever faltering in her flow of words. The question scrawled on the paper asked if we were safe to teleport. I nodded, hoping Dr Thorn hadn't had a breakthrough overnight. Megan sorted out the popcorn and a new movie and closed the curtains of her room so that we could be teleported away in secret.

The scene that greeted me was much the same as it had been last week, with Nuke and Navy waiting in their new lab to talk to me. This time though, there was a new guy with them, a tallish guy, probably not much older than me, with a lean fighter's figure and a mop of brown hair.

"This is Omega," Navy gestured in my direction.

I offered my hand for a shake, "And you are?"

The new guy started to speak, but Navy cut him off, "He hasn't picked a codename yet."

"Yes, I have."

"You can't be called Batman."

I got the feeling that this argument had been going on a while, but Nuke waved them into silence. We had a lot to discuss and only the length of a movie to discuss it. I'm not sure how much Bats knew then about me or my mission inside Grey's Tower. By the end of the next hour he had a much clearer idea. I felt a little awkward discussing all of this in front of a stranger, but questioning Nuke on this, or implying doubt in Bats' loyalty, was probably a bad idea.

I summed up my week, including Jeremy's plans with Dr Thorn. I asked if Jeremy's plan would work.

"Probably," said Navy. "It's how I found Nuke."

Navy and Nuke said that they'd been working on ways to get around it since before my warning, since the first use of Dr Thorn's device. They were able to change the frequency used by the teleporter. Nuke planned to have it work on a shifting pattern so that there was never a fixed frequency to be locked into either for detection or blocking. They were also working on a way to build safe spots that would be shielded from detection. The problem was that something which prevented the signal being picked up might also block the teleport signal.

"Teleporting the journal won't be safe for long," said Nuke, "so I've got a new present."

The new present looked like a sheet of grey plastic about the size of an A4 page. Nuke showed me a similar sheet and a stylus. When Nuke wrote on his sheet, the words appeared on mine. By placing the stylus lengthways and running it down the page, the words were erased from both. We could signal each other much more simply now.

"It's probably best to avoid the girls' nights, as well," Navy said. "Use the mimic sheet if you want to tell us something."

I tucked the sheet and stylus into my handbag.

I explained my plan to continue searching our location list. Nuke nodded, agreeing that it would give the impression of progress without actually doing anything.

Then I told them about Matt.

"He's suspicious about Mrs Grey," I said. "I want to tell him the truth and get him on our side. It would help to have someone else on the inside."

But Nuke wasn't going to risk that. He thought it was too likely that Matt would tell Thomas and that could compromise everything. I was in favour of coming clean to Thomas as well, but that was more my distaste at lying to them. Logically, I had to agree with Nuke's cold strategy. I just didn't have to like it.

What I had to say next was a request. I wanted something to help me spy inside the offices. I didn't understand the technology behind the drone, never mind all the top secret stuff being worked on in the other labs. I wanted a camera of some sort to share the lab's contents with Nuke and Navy. Navy promised to work on it and get me something.

I gave another uncomfortable glance towards Bats and then asked about Knight.

"Same as before," said Princess. "He misses you."

"I miss him too."

"It's not safe for you to see him at the moment," Nuke said. "You're still being observed and any contact with Knight would compromise both your safety and his."

"I know. I just want him to know that I don't like having to stay apart."

"I'll tell him," Princess promised.

I was feeling more uncomfortable about the conversation by the moment, so I turned to Nuke and asked about things with the Guardians.

"We're trying to rebuild our equipment levels to what we had before. Our technology isn't quite at the standard we had, despite Navy's best efforts, but we're being more careful not to let ourselves be quite as vulnerable." He glanced at Bats. "And we're recruiting."

I know that it's common now for some of the Guardians to not know all of the others, but there are more people now and more locations. Back then, with a team of half a dozen, having one be a stranger was disconcerting. Besides, I was feeling frustrated with the whole aura of secrecy. It bothered me that I didn't know Bats's real name or the slightest thing about him. I don't mean any disrespect to him in particular; he's a great Guardian and a phenomenal fighter. But at the time I didn't know that. He was this great big question mark and I was just expected to trust him because Nuke said I should. I think that was the root of my issue: because Nuke said so. Everything came down to his word and I knew nothing more about him than I knew about Bats.

But all I could do was nod and wish him luck, wondering all the while how much he knew about me. He wished me luck in return and then Princess and I prepared to teleport back.

Back in Megan's room, we wrapped up our apparent socialising. I asked if she wanted to meet up next weekend. She made comments about uni work and essays and end-of-module exams. She said she'd text me if she had time. I took this to mean that we should use Navy's gift for updates in future. I found it disproportionally upsetting that I'd be losing my present social life. Megan was hanging out with me because her duty as a Guardian required it, not out of any sense of friendship. Of course, Megan did actually have uni work that her duty to Nuke was already interfering with, but I was in too miserable a mood at the time to consider that. So I just went back to my flat to feel sorry for myself.

Chapter 7

Shortly after my check-in with Nuke and the others, Navy sent me a present. One evening, when I was having a takeaway dinner in my room, I caught a glimpse of a light around the edge of the drawer in which I'd hidden the journal. It shone for a moment and then vanished. Curious, I went to check it out. Lying on balled-up pairs of socks and crumpled knickers was what appeared to be an ordinary USB memory stick.

I slipped it into my handbag and discreetly checked the mimic sheet. There was a long message in Navy's neat handwriting, explaining that the memory stick contained a computer program. It should auto-install if I inserted the stick into a computer and then it would trawl the network for every file I had access to and upload it to a secure location that Navy had set up. I read the message again and this time noticed that there were an awful lot of hesitant words in there. It "should" auto-install. It would "probably" find the files. It would "hopefully" upload them.

I wiped the sheet clean and pointed this out to Navy.

The message came back quickly: *I'm not a computer programmer. "Should" is the best I can manage.*

It didn't fill me with confidence. Still, I'd asked for a weapon in my battle to find information and Navy had provided it. I tucked the memory stick into an inside pocket of my handbag and tried not to think about it for the rest of the evening.

I headed into work early the following morning, the first to arrive in the security office. So far, so good. I got my laptop, made sure it was logged onto the Tower network and inserted the memory stick. In fairness to Navy, the program did do what it was supposed to do and tried to auto-install. Unfortunately, the security software on my laptop also did what it was supposed to do and stopped it. I saw a warning message appear. Apparently, if I wanted the program to install, I could enter an administrator password to authorise it. Too bad I didn't have an administrator password for my laptop and I didn't feel like going to IT support and asking for their help to install a spy program.

I cancelled the warning message and decided to wait until I got back to my flat before using the mimic sheet to explain how the plan had failed.

Minutes later, I was joined in the office by Matt. He was usually one of the first to arrive because Thomas liked to use the gym before work and they travelled in together. He booted up his machine and then went to get coffee.

I had a little spark of an idea. With all the possibly illegal stuff Matt got up to on his computer, it was a safe bet that he had an administrator account. It was also possible that he had access to a lot more than I did on the network, whether he was meant to or not.

I had to act quickly. This brief period of quiet in the office would be the only chance I had to do this unobserved. At least, as unobserved as I could be. I was still aware of the secure camera in the corner of the office and my mysterious watchers. I couldn't just use Matt's computer without it looking suspicious. I needed an excuse.

While he was getting his coffee, I quickly checked I could open the memory stick as a folder and dumped a file of notes into it. I then deleted the default printer from my settings.

When Matt came back, I was muttering insults at my computer that it wanted to send my notes to OneNote instead of printing them out.

Matt gave a sigh, "What's wrong?"

"The stupid thing won't print," I complained. "Can I use yours for a sec just to print something out?"

"Sure," he said. "Let me check what you've done to yours."

He unplugged the power cable from his laptop and handed it over to me. I passed him mine with clammy hands. While he was delving into settings to find the fault, I stuck the memory stick into the USB port of his machine. A warning flashed up on screen asking for authorisation, but this time it didn't require a password. I accepted it the instant it appeared, glancing across at Matt. He was still focused on my printer settings and didn't notice. I breathed again.

I opened up my notes and set them to print, wondering how long it would take for Navy's program to install.

I walked to the printer and by the time I'd returned, Matt had solved my supposed error and reclaimed his laptop. He pulled out the USB stick. I had no way of knowing if it had been in there long enough to do its job. I just tucked it back into my handbag and politely listened to Matt explain how to add a printer to my machine if I managed to delete the settings again.

"I'm still not sure how I did that."

Matt just shook his head, "You're worse than Thomas."

I had to exercise patience and pretend to work on my notes, talking to the others when they came in. It was over an hour later when I was able to slip out to the ladies. While shut in a cubical and hopefully safe from any cameras, I risked a glance at the mimic sheet. Navy reported that the program had started uploading files.

***

Over the course of the day, Navy's little spy program uploaded vast quantities of the files that Matt's computer could access from the Grey's Tower network, saving them to the site Navy had set up for the purpose. Matt complained several times about how slowly the network was running, asking if we were having problems. He even joked that I'd cursed his machine when I'd used it.

It was hard to laugh at that.

When he moaned and said that he'd have to run diagnostics on it when he got some time, I had to fight down the urge to panic. If he found that program he'd probably be able to check when it was installed and he'd know it had to be me. My cover would be blown, he'd never trust me again and Navy's program would be stopped before it could finish copying all the files.

Strangely, it was the middle one of those that worried me the most. I didn't want him to know that I'd tricked him, that I'd betrayed him. These guys were my friends. Sort of. Nearly. I wanted to be part of the group. Yet here I was, faking a laugh and pretending to belong, knowing that I was lying to them with every breath.

***

I checked the mimic sheet again when I was safely at home, with the curtains shut and the sheet tucked inside my journal, so even if someone was watching me, it wouldn't be immediately obvious. It was Nuke's handwriting that replied, saying that Navy was busy catching up on work for the university. Nuke reported that the upload had given them terabytes of files to work through. There was a vast amount of content so he wasn't certain what they had found yet. A lot of it was clearly mundane, including emails to family members, or time sheet reporting. There was a lot that he hadn't had a chance to check yet but, most promising of all, apparently there were several folders of encrypted files.

It will take some time to crack the encryptions, Nuke wrote, *but the security on them would suggest that we've managed to get something important.*

I should have been happy with that. I ought to have been pleased that my work had uncovered something that we could use to determine Mrs Grey's true purpose with the Tower. But encrypted files were really no more useful than having nothing. The pessimistic bit of my brain said that we were no better off than before I'd begun my infiltration.

Nuke hadn't finished writing. He commented that he was surprised about how much I'd had access to. I explained about using Matt's computer.

That's very risky, Nuke wrote. *He might notice the program.*

It wouldn't install on mine! I wrote back. I was in no mood to argue about it with him because I'd achieved the goal even when Navy's program hadn't quite worked as planned. I'd probably got more information than would have been possible from my computer. It felt like Nuke was criticising me, which in my current mood just riled me.

I bit down on my anger, wiped the mimic sheet clean and went out to get some dinner.

Chapter 8

"I've got something!"

I'd only just walked in the door one morning when Matt grabbed me and pulled me over to his desk. Thomas, who'd been sitting talking to Matt, nodded me a greeting. Matt, grinning like a kid with a new toy, started talking rapidly.

"It was bothering me," he said, "that your Ethan guy was never reported missing. No police, no upset, no requests for information. That just doesn't happen. So I started looking into his university records." I didn't ask about the legalities of this. I also didn't question that he'd referred to Ethan as mine.

"He's been turning up to seminars," Matt went on, "handing in assignments, meeting with his tutor. He's still going to university. So I accessed the campus CCTV and tracked back his movement from his seminars. He's teleporting into the toilets. Either that or he's got one hell of a case of constipation."

I felt a cold weight in my stomach. After being so careful to keep away from Ethan, he was still in danger. I wanted to call him, to warn him of the threat. More than that, I wanted to beg Matt to ignore what he'd found, to just forget about it. I'd come to think of Matt and Thomas as friends. I hated the thought of them hunting for Ethan as an enemy.

"Are you OK?" Thomas asked. I must have been standing there like a lemon.

I nodded. "What do we do with this information? The university's too public for a confrontation. He's obviously confident that we can't get to him there."

"We can't just charge in with guns and grab him," Thomas agreed, "but we can still get information from him."

"How?" I asked.

"How about the direct approach? We ask him. A confrontation with an ex-girlfriend could give us some insights into what's really going on." Thomas was looking at me significantly.

I couldn't do this.

"Or send him running for the hills," I said. "Maybe we should keep our distance and observe, see who he interacts with."

"Maybe you could try to get close to him?" suggested Matt. "Pretend to be the distraught girlfriend. Say you want to know what he's planning because you can't believe he's a criminal."

I couldn't quite believe that I was facing the possibility of working for Nuke, pretending to work for Mrs Grey, pretending to work for Nuke. It would end up far too confusing. There were already too many secrets, too many lies and bluffs, for me to keep track of how I should be acting. I needed to stop this and, for once, I decided that the truth was the simplest option.

"I'm not sure I'm up to that," I said. "Ethan... I... I don't think I can face him."

"Which is what makes this perfect," Thomas insisted. "A part of you still likes him. Admit it." I looked away. "You're genuinely conflicted, so if you go and talk to him he'll drink it up. Maybe he'll spill some of his secrets to get you on his side."

"He knows I work here. He won't buy it."

I was still trying to think of a way to refuse to carry out this plan that would withstand arguments. The problem was... it was a good plan. I was in a perfect position to play double agent. Too bad I already was. When Chris joined us and heard the summary of the discussion, he was instantly in agreement with Thomas. By this point, others were coming into the office in dribs and drabs. Chris looked over to where Damian was hanging up his coat and turning on his computer.

"We want to get information quickly," Chris pointed out.

"But not at the risk of losing a potential source of more information," I argued again. "Maybe we can find some way to track Ethan when he teleports away."

"You want to talk to Dr Thorn about that?" asked Chris. He gave another meaningful look towards Damian.

In the end, I had to acquiesce. The guys were giving me sympathetic looks but it seemed that protecting the raw emotions of the one girl in the team wasn't a high priority for them. I couldn't keep protesting without feeling whiny and weak.

"Fine," I said, "but we're doing this my way."

Matt had pulled up Ethan's university schedule as well as video footage of his recent visits to campus. From these, we plotted his likely behaviour.

"He's got a seminar tomorrow morning," Matt said, "on the first floor of Vanbrugh College." Matt spent some time on the university website trying find a building plan before giving up and scribbling a rough diagram on a piece of paper. I found it both amusing and worrying that this guy could break into secure video footage more easily than he could find a map.

"This is the room where he has his seminar," Matt said, pointing to a wobbly rectangle. "These are the stairs. This is the gents. Based on what's he's done before, he'll teleport into the toilets sometime between quarter to and ten, when they're empty. He'll go to his ten o'clock seminar. Afterwards, he'll go straight back to the toilets and teleport out."

"That doesn't give me much time to confront him," I said.

"True," said Matt. "And there are likely to be other people around. But that's probably a good thing."

We spent the whole morning planning. We discussed, debated and described all options until we knew exactly what everyone else was going to be doing. I was the only one allowed to improvise. The others would be waiting and watching, ready to intervene in case of danger. I would, of course, be wired up. Every word Ethan and I said to each other would be recorded for later dissection. Matt would be in charge of that, waiting nearby and observing electronically. Thomas and Chris would be close at hand, ready to step in if things went wrong.

The afternoon was spent kitting up. Chris took me through the official equipment requisitioning process. There were various forms on the intranet we had to fill out to get hold of the surveillance gear we'd be using, but from the middle of the afternoon the mailroom staff started bringing in boxes of electronics for us to sign for.

Across the office, Jeremy and Damian were watching us. I don't know what they thought we were up to. They were dipping in and out to have meetings with various members of the science staff. I was certainly intrigued about what they were up to and how near they were to being able to track the teleporting. I was tempted to try testing out our newly-acquired surveillance gear on them to see what we could learn.

While we were doing our official planning, I was thinking over how I should handle this. I kept mulling over different approaches I could take. If we were careful, then we could use this meeting to convince my unseen watchers that I wasn't working with Nuke's team, while stirring up Matt's doubts to try and win him and the others to our cause.

When I got home from work late that evening, I tucked the mimic sheet inside my journal and filled it up with small writing as I explained that Ethan had been discovered, what we were planning, and how I wanted Ethan to react. Ethan and I would have to act out our parts for our various audiences.

***

We arrived on campus at about ten o'clock, Matt parking one of the Grey's Tower vans in the central campus car park. He set up the equipment in the back and we tested the multiple microphones I had concealed under my winter coat. The campus was covered with an icy drizzle while a bitter wind blew from the north, so no one would question my choosing to wear a garment bulky enough to conceal the audio transmitters, as well as a couple of weapons. They were non-lethal weapons; apparently Matt's dubious practices regarding legalities only applied to what he got up to on the computer. I had a mini version of the glue gun in one pocket. It probably wouldn't be enough to immobilise a person, but could mess them up if they were trying to attack me. I also had a small tranquiliser gun in my other pocket.

Thomas and Chris were also armed. Thomas had made use of his sports bag to hide the full-sized glue gun. If we were flooded with Nuke's Guardians, he'd be able to immobilise them while we made a run for the van. At least that was the theory. I wasn't expecting a fight today. When I'd woken up, after spending half the night tossing and turning, my message had been wiped clear from the mimic sheet and replaced with a simple reply from Navy saying that they understood and would follow my lead.

Around the time the seminar would be halfway through, the three of us left the van. Chris would linger in an empty seminar room a little down the corridor. Thomas would be waiting at the bottom of the stairs. Both were fitted with earpieces to hear whatever I said. I checked my own earpiece as I walked away from the van.

"You'll be OK," Matt muttered in my ear. "We're right here with you."

"Thanks," I muttered back. The other two shot me confused looks; apparently Matt had only been talking on my channel.

I headed for the stairs and through a door into the corridor where I was meant to wait. As we arrived, Chris gave me a reassuring smile before going to wait in the other room as planned. I checked the room numbers on the door and then waited, standing outside the door of the seminar room for Ethan to appear.

It was strangely quiet. I could hear faint murmurs of voices through the doors, occasionally rising in volume enough for me to pick out whole words. At one point there was a burst of laughter from one room, but, in general, it was just a background hum. No one seemed to be about, apart from those on the other side of the doors in the various seminars. The most exciting point of my wait was when a guy came through a door from where the English department had their offices and walked past me towards the toilets. He came back a few minutes later drying his hands on his jeans. For the rest of my wait, all I could do was think and fret.

It should have been easy. All I had to do was talk. Ethan and I had our roles to play and then we'd go our separate ways. I knew he wasn't going to fight me. I knew that I was perfectly safe. So why was I more scared than when we'd raided Grey's Tower?

I hadn't seen Ethan since that night in the warehouse. A part of me wanted to run rather than see him now, but the rest of me was waiting desperately for that first glimpse. I wanted to look into his eyes and see if he still cared or if I was just some brief fling already forgotten. I tried to push those thoughts aside. I had a job to do. Whatever spark Ethan and I might have had, he'd broken our fledgling relationship off. Right now, I had to focus on proving to Mrs Grey, or whoever it was she had spying on me, that I wasn't working with Nuke's forces.

I kept glancing at my watch, wondering idly if Navy had come up with something that slowed down time because there was no way it should be taking this long. At last, one of the other doors opened and a flow of students came out, chatting, gathering up notes, or bundling up into layers of warm clothes for the journey across campus. I still waited, standing across from Ethan's seminar room, fighting the urge to run.

"Any minute now," I muttered under my breath. It didn't cause so much as a glance my way from the passing students, but I got a faint response in my ear.

"We're ready," said Thomas.

After a few moments, the noise level rose behind the door I was watching and then it opened, spewing forth its mass of students. The first few passed without seeming to notice me. Then Ethan stepped out and stopped short, causing a girl to nearly crash into him from behind. Ethan's face showed an impressively believable look of surprise. Only I was looking closely enough to see that it came a fraction of a second too late.

"Jenny!" The tone of voice was as convincing as the expression.

That was good. That was what I'd wanted. But I couldn't help wonder whether his emotions during our times together had been as easily faked.

"Hi, Ethan," I said, instantly realizing how unimpressive that was as a greeting.

The girl forced her way past Ethan, who was still half-blocking the doorway. He seemed to come out of a daze and stepped aside, letting the rest of his seminar group leave. We stood in the corridor for a moment. To anyone watching, this would appear to be the awkward confrontation between two recently-dating individuals.

"We've got a lot of stuff to talk about," I said.

"Yeah. Um. I guess." He ran a hand through his hair. His other hand was clutching the strap of a backpack which he had over one shoulder. We stood awkwardly for a moment longer, then another door opened and a line of students tried to make their way past us to the stairs. Others were already heading up in preparation for the next set of seminars. We were rather blocking the flow.

"Maybe we should go somewhere more private," Ethan said.

"Actually, public works for me," I answered.

"Right. Of course. Well, downstairs maybe?"

I agreed, partly because I'd just been bumped by the third person who was trying to get past me in the busy corridor. Downstairs was the Union bar. The bar wasn't as crowded as it would be at the lunchtime rush, but there were plenty of people buying snacks or drinks, or sitting at the small tables. It was certainly public enough. We passed Thomas on the way down and, as we walked into the bar, I spotted another familiar face. Adam was sitting at a corner table, various papers spread out over it, weighed down by a book as thick as my fist. His eyes flickered towards us for a moment, but then he returned to his papers. Wearing a t-shirt on which a stick figure declared loudly that 'science worked', and reading his physics book, he was a lot less conspicuous than the two guys who were surveying for my side. No one could possibly guess that he was codename Navy, one of Nuke's team.

We found an empty table between Adam's and a trio of maths

students working on an assignment over coffee. We sat there like civilised people, hiding in plain sight. I heard Matt's voice mutter in my ear to check for exits and I glanced round despite myself, taking in the main exit beside Adam. Behind me, just beyond the maths students, was a way out into the Vanbrugh common room, from which I could hear the blare of the TV and some people arguing about pool. There might have been another way out through the lecture hall to the left, I wasn't sure. I wasn't too worried though; it wasn't like Adam or Ethan were about to hurt me.

"How've you been?" Ethan asked. I could have laughed at the absurd normality of the question.

"Pretty much recovered from the smoke inhalation now," I said. I didn't try to keep the bitterness from my tone.

"Are you... um... were you hurt?"

"A bit."

"Oh. Sorry."

The awkwardness dragged out. Ethan glanced across at the three maths students, debating something about differentials. They didn't seem to be paying any attention to us, but there was still an issue of secrecy we both had to respect.

"You said you didn't know I was involved in this," he said.

"I didn't. Not until... you know. Did you?"

"No."

Across the room, Adam glanced up long enough from his papers to roll his eyes. Presumably he was waiting for us to get on with a real conversation.

"Are you still working for the same company?" Ethan asked.

"Yes. They've been very good to me. They helped me a lot after our... split."

"You shouldn't trust them."

"So, should I trust the people who left me tied up in a burning warehouse over the people who rescued me from it?" That was said for the benefit of the various Grey's Tower people listening in, but the bitterness caused Ethan to look away, guilt on his face.

"One of your people killed Professor Swinson," I continued. This was one of the things I'd included in my instructions to Navy, one element of truth I wanted my colleagues to hear. Ethan managed a realistic expression of surprise.

"That's a lie," Ethan said. "He was already dead. Someone inside Grey's Tower killed him."

I saw Adam glance up, looking towards the maths students. They didn't seem to be paying us the slightest bit of attention, but we dropped our voices again.

"Why the hell would anyone in the Tower hurt him?"

"I don't know. That's a question you should ask your boss."

"Why should I believe you?" I knew it was true because I'd been the one to find Swinson's body. But my eavesdroppers didn't know that and if I wanted them to believe I wasn't working with Nuke's team, I needed to put myself apart from them.

"We're not the bad guys here," Ethan said, his voice low again, aware of another group of people walking past us, heading to the bar. They paid us no more attention than anyone else.

"Then give me answers," I said. I wasn't sure how much Ethan would admit, knowing that everything he said was being recorded. Whatever he said to convince Matt and the others was being heard by whoever else it was following me and might well end up at Mrs Grey's ears. But Ethan nodded, prepared to make revelations.

"We call ourselves the Guardians because we stop threats," he said. "You know about Victor and Casey. Well, they found a meteor. Just a little lump of rock. It nearly killed them both. There were organic elements in the meteor, a few single-celled organisms. They were resilient little buggers that managed to survive the fall through the atmosphere and wanted somewhere to grow. They infected Victor first, but they spread to others, including Casey. Nuke poured his everything into finding the cure. He saved them both, stopped a plague before it became anything more than an anomalous fever."

Looking into Ethan's eyes, I knew that every word he said was true. This was why he followed Nuke so faithfully, why he trusted this man neither of us knew anything about. I wished I could believe Nuke the hero so easily. I still do. Even now, when I've seen exactly how much Nuke was willing to sacrifice, I doubt his motives. Everything he did with the Guardians was wonderful, but I still want to know why.

"You're not actually buying this, are you?" That was Chris's voice in my ear. He was somewhere nearby, listening to the same story. So much for my hope that my colleagues would be enlightened by this endeavour. I had to push harder.

"Then why the thefts?" I asked. My voice was barely above a whisper. Behind me, the maths students were packing up, with two of them heading over to the bar and the other walking out the door. It didn't take long for them to be replaced by a couple coming over with sandwiches. A part of me wanted to laugh that we could talk in so public a place about all of this, within reach of people leading ordinary oblivious lives.

"That technology is way beyond anything that should be developed on Earth and extremely dangerous in the wrong hands," Ethan said.

"And what right do you have to decide whose hands are right?"

"I trust Nuke. If you can give me a good reason why Mrs Grey needs a power source that could blow up half the country, I'm listening."

This was meant to be an act, but it had stopped feeling like it. It felt like the argument was real and I wanted to defend my suspicions about Nuke, even though I trusted Mrs Grey even less. I remembered the conversations I'd had in Swinson's lab, the things he'd get excited about when he talked about his work.

"Swinson was interested in clean energy," I answered. "Maybe Mrs Grey wanted to use the quantum thingy to solve the global warming issues."

"Or she's building weapons."

"Yeah, to stop alien threats." That came out in a hissed whisper so we weren't overheard. I had to lean across the table for him to hear and he leaned towards me. I felt my heart rate jump up a gear, as he was so close, right in front of me. For a moment, I wanted to throw the act aside, forget our argument and just close what little distance was left.

I wanted to kiss him. Maybe he saw my desire because he looked away, pulling back and leaning on one arm of his chair so that his body was now slightly tilted away from me. He still wanted distance from me and that damn near broke my heart again.

I needed to focus. I needed to get things back on track and wrap this up because I was about to have a meltdown. I closed my eyes for a moment and breathed deeply, bringing myself back to the plan. When I looked back at Ethan, he was still looking away from me, blinking rapidly as though he too were fighting tears.

"Your boss," I said quietly, "has access to technology that just isn't possible for him to have. The things he's got, the things he can do, just don't make sense. As far as Grey's Tower is concerned, you guys are an alien threat and I'm not sure they're wrong."

Ethan gave a bitter laugh, "Do I look alien?"

"No. Of course not. But what about Nuke?"

"What?"

"Can you be sure he's human?"

"I..." Ethan trailed of. He couldn't answer me.

Chapter 9

I escaped to the van soon after that. Ethan said he had places to be. I knew that we'd arranged for the meeting to end like this, but a part of me still wondered if he just didn't want to face that last question I'd asked. He slipped away and I followed suit a moment later, walking past Adam's sympathetic glance and out to the car park. Thomas fell into stride beside me and placed a hand on my shoulder.

I made it back to the van before breaking down completely. Sat on the floor of the van, beside Matt and his surveillance gear, I started sobbing uncontrollably. I could only hope that Matt had turned off the recording before that started.

The logical part of me tried to gain control, insisting that I barely knew Ethan. It shouldn't matter to me that he'd pulled away. It shouldn't bother me that our act had felt real. It shouldn't matter, but it did. I wanted him to look at me and smile the way he had when we'd had our first date. I wanted to throw all acts aside and just beg his forgiveness for having worked against him, however unintentionally.

But we both had a job to do first.

The others let me cry. They sat around me awkwardly. At one point, someone tried patting my back in what was presumably meant to be a comforting way. As the sobs slowed and I got myself under control again, Chris handed me some toilet roll to wipe my face with and blow my nose. I hadn't even noticed him come in.

"Don't make me go through that again," I said. Matt tried the awkward pat-on-the-back thing again.

"It's over," Thomas said.

"But we did learn something useful," Chris said. "He definitely wants Jenny on his side. That was the hard sell."

"He believed every word," I said.

"Which prompts some interesting questions," said Matt. "Particularly about Professor Swinson. I still haven't managed to find any footage about his death."

I resisted the urge to say something. Matt might have turned off his recording, but someone else out there was still spying on me. I couldn't be sure that whatever I said now wouldn't be used against me by Mrs Grey.

Despite my state, I was aware of the look passing between the other occupants of the van. A look which said that something important had just happened. The others looked to me. I looked away.

***

Back at the office, we had analysis to do. Matt wanted to go over all of Ethan's statements to look for any vital clues we might have missed the first time round. I started to sit through the recording, but hearing Ethan's voice again stung. I ended up excusing myself and having a little cry in the toilets.

I was ashamed of myself for this reaction. I was supposed to be strong, supposed to be helping uncover the truth about this organisation, but all I wanted to do was run and hide like a little girl. The strength of my own feelings overwhelmed me. I'd only dated Ethan a couple of weeks and this reaction seemed ridiculous. I forced myself to calm down and return to the office.

Thomas was the one who suggested that maybe I should take the afternoon off. Somehow, the sympathy just made me feel more ashamed. It made me feel weak and I hated that.

I forced myself to stay, partly because I didn't really have anywhere else to be. I did separate myself from the others slightly by heading to my own laptop and opening up my email. Then I spent some time continuing the analysis into potential locations for Nuke's new base. After an hour or so, Thomas declared it time for a coffee break. He pulled me from the office, Matt and Chris trailing along too.

We headed to a little coffee shop on Castlegate that was apparently Thomas's favourite. Wrapped up in winter coats, we set out into streets that were crowded with Christmas shoppers, despite it being a weekday. On the walk, Matt pulled out a sheet of paper and handed it to me. It was a printout of a newspaper article he must have found on the web, something from a local paper.

I instantly recognised the pair in the picture. The twins, Victor and Casey, otherwise known as Victory and Valiant, smiled out of the photo, holding what looked like a lump of rock between them. The headline talked about their "Out Of This World Discovery". It seemed the article was reporting on the twins finding a meteor in a field near their village.

"I accessed hospital records," Matt said. "There were several cases of unexplained fever shortly after this. The source was never identified and the patients' recovery was ascribed to a broad spectrum antibiotic, but there was never really an explanation."

"So Ethan was telling the truth," I said.

"Looks that way," he said.

I was aware of the fact that I might be still observed. It was obvious that they'd brought me out here because they wanted to have the conversation where we wouldn't be caught on camera or overheard by others in Tower security. I was torn. Should I let this conversation carry on and talk to them about how Ethan genuinely was one of the good guys? Or should I keep playing the part of someone loyal to Grey's Tower? I was sick of the lies and unsure what good I was doing for Nuke anyway.

"Do you think he was telling the truth about the rest of it?" Matt asked. The question was directed at me. The other two were listening for my answer. I kept my gaze down, focusing on dodging between laden shoppers.

"I want to believe him," I admitted. I remembered the conversation I'd once had with Professor Swinson and tried to use what we'd discussed then to hedge now.

"Maybe this is all some horrible mistake," I went on. "Maybe we should all be on the same side but things have got muddled and now we're fighting each other. Maybe if we could get both sides to sit down and just talk then this would all be over."

"That's a lot of maybes," said Chris.

I nodded.

We reached the coffee shop. Thomas treated me to a camomile tea that was supposed to help me calm down, but I didn't feel particularly calm. I ordered a muffin too, picking it apart with my fingers and eating little bites. I chose it mostly so that I could put something in my mouth so I'd have an excuse not to answer right away when the others spoke. I could feel the wall of secrets around me again, separating me from these supposed friends who were trying so hard to be nice to me. I was close to another breakdown.

We couldn't really linger, so it was back out into the cold streets, heading back to the office with our drinks clutched in our hands. I was in no hurry to get back to work, but I walked quickly, weaving through the crowds. Partly it was because of a desire to get out of the cold, but mostly I just wanted a reason not to look at the others.

I was feeling more of a fraud than ever. Even then I was wondering about just coming clean and telling them what I knew, but I wasn't sure that would help. If I admitted the truth, then it would mean admitting that I'd set up the conversation with Ethan. They might be less likely to come round than if I left them believing the lie of my allegiance.

We'd barely got back to our respective desks when Lucy came to find us. She wanted to talk to us about what we'd learned from Ethan. I was astonished, almost scared, that she knew before we'd even had a chance to report it. It probably shouldn't have been so shocking. Grey's Tower was her world. She knew everyone and everything within its walls. No doubt she'd seen the equipment requests and known our plan and now she'd observed our quick trip out and return, coming to summon us into a meeting room.

Across the room, Damian was looking towards us and grinning. No doubt he thought we were about to be berated for lack of progress.

We gave a summary of our plans to Lucy, with Chris doing most of the talking as he explained what we'd achieved. I found myself fidgeting constantly with the necklace that Navy had given me. I half-wanted to escape, to send the emergency signal. It was comforting to know that I had this tool, a way to get out if this went as wrong as I was scared it might.

Chris and Matt talked about my encounter with Ethan and what they'd recorded. Lucy listened intently, sitting up sharply when they reached Ethan's comment about Grey's Tower being another alien threat. I made myself look up from the table at that point, seeing the expression on Lucy's face. She was clearly surprised, a faint smile on her lips as though the concept was laughable. I supposed that was a good sign.

"I would be intrigued to hear the recordings," Lucy said.

Chris agreed instantly.

Lucy leaned her elbows on the table, lacing her fingers together as she looked round the table at each of us in turn. I tried to still my fidgeting fingers, hoping I didn't look too nervous.

"What will you do next?" she asked. I felt three pairs of eyes flick in my direction. There was a pause, as though everyone expected me to speak. That moment seemed to drag for an eternity.

"We keep going with our original plan," said Chris, "to locate their new base. But in the meantime, we keep watch on Ethan. He's unlikely to interact with the others at the university, but we can still track his actions just in case. I think trying to bring him in or question him would cause more problems than it's worth."

"I expect that you're right," Lucy said. "Bringing him here before cost us a lot, cost us good people. We can't risk another attack like that until we are better able to defend ourselves. Dr Thorn has a prototype ready for testing to track the teleportation signals. If you work on narrowing the list of potential sites for their base, he will be able to test much more effectively than via a manual search."

My blood froze at her words and I had to fight to keep breathing normally. My fingers tightened momentarily on the metal circle of the necklace. I forced my hand to relax and managed a smile. I think

I even managed to say something as we wrapped up the meeting, some bland comment about how it was good that we were closing in.

I got out of the office as soon as I reasonably could, even though the others looked set for a late night working. I couldn't take it anymore.

I hurried home, feeling my emotions, my fears, surging inside me. I felt like a fragile shell trying to hold inside a war of thoughts. It seemed I could crack at any moment.

Back in my little flat, shutting curtains against any potential watchers outside, I wrote a warning on the mimic sheet, telling Navy and the others that the teleport tracker was almost ready. Thankfully, it sounded like it was still short-range, so Dr Thorn wasn't going to find their base unless we inadvertently brought him close. Even so, this could mean big trouble for Megan and Adam. They had lives and work and studies here. If they couldn't teleport in secret, they would be effectively trapped. My brain whirled with near panic on their behalf, as well as fears of my own exposure.

Sat in my room, unable to focus on any task in my current state, it occurred to me that I'd barely eaten all day. The thought of cooking was effort beyond my current mind-set so I placed a takeaway order. When the food arrived, I was able to shut down my brain for a short while. The simple act of bringing a fork to my mouth gave me a focus and brought to a stop that raging terror within. But when the food was gone, the thoughts were still there, lurking, waiting for me.

I ended up going to the little shop round the corner and buying some snacks for dessert, just so I could keep eating longer. As long as I was putting biscuits in my mouth, I wasn't thinking about Ethan or Mrs Grey or Nuke or any of the problems that were waiting for me.

I couldn't eat forever.

I sat on my bed, tears trickling down my face and dripping onto empty biscuit packets and takeaway boxes. I was, once again, that fragile shell about to crack. Filling myself up with food hadn't made the problem go away. It had just made me feel sick as well as scared and miserable.

I couldn't keep this up.

That was the moment it crystallised in my mind. I wasn't cut out for this whole double agent thing. I couldn't keep going with the lies and secrets. For the sake of my sanity, I had to walk away.

With new resolve, I fished out my mimic sheet, which still bore the message I'd written earlier that evening. At the bottom of the sheet, I wrote more lines.

I want out. I can't keep doing this and I'm not finding anything useful. I want to come clean.

Having done that, I prepared for bed and attempted to get my thoughts to shut up long enough for me to get a couple of hours sleep.

Chapter 10

I barely slept that night, my thoughts still racing. Guilt over backing out was chasing in circles with the fears of what might happen if I kept up the act. I dozed and woke. My fears slipped into nightmares that brought me sweating back to waking. Sometime in the early hours, I was woken for good by an unmistakeable line of light showing around the edge of one of my drawers. Someone had just teleported me a present.

I gave up on my bed and I found a reply on the mimic sheet. Nuke wanted me to go back in one last time and try and find out what I could about Mrs Grey's plans. If I wasn't going to stay working at the Tower, then subtlety was no longer an issue. I should learn anything I could and then get out of there, using the emergency signal if I ran into trouble. The present turned out to be a watch that apparently had a camera behind the face. All I had to do was point it and it would record everything for Navy and Nuke to analyse later. I was to go into the Tower and access every part I could get away with, recording every last detail.

If I could bluff my way in as a Tower employee, it would buy me more time to find out more. If I was caught, I could signal and they'd teleport me to safety. If something went wrong, then I might have to defend myself.

There was a second part to the gift I'd been sent, something that was already mine. Nuke had sent me one of the alien guns that matched my Omega armour. If the worst came to the worst, I had something to protect myself with.

Sleep was out of the question, so I took a long shower and prepared myself for the day. I dressed in my usual work clothes, opting for trousers instead of a skirt today and flats over heels. If I ended up getting caught, I was going to be wearing something in which I could fight. I clipped my hair up in what was both a suitable style for a professional and a good way to keep it out of my eyes if things went wrong. I applied a light touch of make-up to disguise the shadows under my eyes from the sleepless night and then I was ready. I inspected myself in the mirror and saw a young businesswoman dressed plainly but smartly for the day ahead.

I wondered briefly if anyone else in the world was choosing their work attire based on how easy it would be to fight in. In my sleep-deprived state, that struck me as funny, but I was too nervous to laugh.

I put on the signal jewellery and the new watch, making sure that it sat low enough on my wrist that the face wouldn't be covered by the sleeve of my jacket. Then I packed my bag for the day, slipping the gun and the mimic sheet into my handbag, first checking that the gun was definitely powered off. I didn't want it to catch on something and accidentally shoot my own leg.

I hesitated for a while. It was still early, ridiculously early, so I tried to think of anything else I could do to prepare. I kept thinking of Matt and his doubts. He'd been the one who'd verified the story about Valiant and Victory. He'd been the one suspicious about Professor Swinson's death. I wanted to give him something.

So I ripped a page out of my barely-used journal and wrote a note. It was simple enough, just stating that Professor Swinson had been killed before the attack on the Tower because he'd discovered something about Mrs Grey's plans. I didn't admit to working with Nuke, I just stuck to those basic facts. I tucked the note into my handbag so that I could leave it somewhere for him to find. I wondered whether I should write a message for Chris and Thomas too, but figured one would be enough.

Then I had no other way to stall. I could procrastinate in my flat for a little longer, but I wanted to get this over with, so I pulled on my various layers and walked out into the cold street. It was raining, with that thin, misty drizzle that somehow managed to soak me in moments. I had to hope that the watch Navy had built was waterproof, but I didn't have any way to check that it was actually working. I just slunk my way through the rain between sleeping shops until I reached Grey's Tower.

One guy stood on duty at the front door, sheltering against the wall, out of the rain. He nodded to me as I swiped my badge.

"Lucy working you guys all hours again?" he asked.

I gave a vaguely affirmative answer and then was inside. The receptionist hadn't arrived yet and my feet clomped loudly against the polished floor as I made my way to the lift. I began to wish that I'd waited until normal office hours to make things less suspicious, but I was committed now. I let myself up to the security offices and then went to my desk. I powered on the computer like it was any other workday, hanging up my coat and scarf in the usual place. I even made a point of skimming my email, just in case anyone was watching and checking up on my behaviour.

A few minutes after my arrival, I went over to Matt's desk, looking through various printouts that scattered the surface. He'd found a few more articles about the mysterious illness that had struck shortly after the twins' meteor discovery. I read them, genuinely interested, and then sorted through for the transcript of my conversation with Ethan.

While I was sorting through papers, it was a simple matter to slip the note under his keyboard so that just a corner was poking out. It wouldn't be too obvious, but Matt should see it when he sat down to start his own day.

All the while, I made sure that the watch face was uncovered. During the course of various, seemingly-ordinary movements, I pointed it in each direction in turn, ensuring that the entire security office would be on the footage. But there was more to record.

I was heading for the door when it opened. To my dismay, Damian walked into the room, the dripping umbrella in his hand evidence of his recent journey into work. He looked at me with instant suspicion.

"What the hell are you doing here?"

"My job," I replied.

He didn't seem convinced, but staying and trying to convince him would probably make him more suspicious than just brushing him off, so I walked past him as though I had every right in the world to be doing so.

My first stop was the storage area where we'd gotten the surveillance gear. The rooms made up about a quarter of a floor, with a little office housing sign-out sheets for brief loans as well as the computer for logging longer-term borrowing on the system. This was where my laptop had come from when I'd first arrived and this was where earpieces and transmitters lived, boxed away and barcoded.

There was no one in the office yet, but I was able to boot up the computer and use my own password to access it. I skimmed through the lists of equipment, leaning my elbow on the desk so that the watch was pointed at the computer screen. Most of this stuff was perfectly ordinary, with computers and peripherals, printer parts and spare projectors available in case any of the equipment in a meeting room broke down. There was the surveillance gear with microphones, transmitters, cameras and enough spy toys to observe half a town. Then came the scientific stuff. I had no idea what half of the names meant, but I carefully ran down the list and made sure I'd recorded it all. Hopefully it would mean more to Navy than to me.

It took me about twenty minutes to go through all the lists because I wasn't exactly reading them carefully. Nothing jumped out as being world-threatening. I wondered about trying to get into the store rooms to see if anything was out of place, but I decided not to bother. It wasn't like I'd recognise half of the lab equipment anyway. Just in case anyone asked what I was doing here, I made a point of looking up the record of our borrowing yesterday to check that everything had been signed back in properly.

The next stage was more difficult and more dangerous. I had to get into the labs. If anything secret was going on, that would be where to find it. But half of the building was labs and I'd seen little beyond Professor Swinson's. I wondered about starting there but was convinced that Swinson at least hadn't been working on anything that would threaten the planet, so I went for Dr Thorn's instead. If I was cornered, I could at least bluff something about talking to him about his teleport tracker progress.

I tried my access card at the door to the lab, but the little light on the lock flashed red at me. I wasn't authorised to go in. I was just debating whether to fish the gun out of the bag and cut my way in when the door opened. A lab tech looked out at me. He'd clearly heard me at the door and now he stood in the doorway, blocking my way in.

"Can I help you with something?" His tone was friendly but his body language clearly articulated that he wasn't about to let me inside. Fortunately, I could at least point the face of my watch around his body to get some footage of the lab.

I did my best to smile and act calmly. "I was wondering if Dr Thorn was in yet?"

"Not yet. He usually gets in about half-eight, but give him a chance to get some coffee before you come back or he'll probably bite your head off."

"Got it. Thanks."

I made a point of checking my watch, which allowed me to move my arm around to get some different angles around the lab tech's body. Then the door was slammed in my face.

There were other labs on the same floor, but they were locked to me as well. I could break into one, but the minute I tried that, my cover would be blown. So I played the infiltration card once more. The only other lab I had a connection with was the one we'd borrowed the unmanned drone from. I went there now, trying to remember the name of the researcher we'd spoken to at the time. I needn't have bothered with that because I never made it to the lab.

Damian was waiting by the lifts for me. He was leaning against the wall, arms folded, an image of calm patience.

"Care to tell me what you're doing?" he asked. His tone was casual but I picked up the note of threat behind it.

"I thought I'd pick Dr Thorn's brain about the teleporting," I said, "but I guess I'm a bit early."

It didn't sound convincing even to my ears.

"You're not fooling anyone, love."

I reached up for the necklace, hoping he thought it was just a nervous fidget. But how to get an earring out without it being obvious?

"I don't know what you mean," I stalled.

"Oh, give it up! No one's buying your sweet innocent routine. Do you really think we believe you just happened to escape from them?"

"I didn't escape. I nearly burned to death." I had the pendant in my hand, but I needed the earring to send the signal. I didn't think I could do it without him seeing so I just had to be quick.

"You had it all figured out, didn't you?" Damian kept talking. He was closing the distance between us, getting uncomfortably close. I took a step backwards just to get some space back and then regretted it instantly. Backing away from him made it look like I was guilty.

"You thought you could play the victim and have us all eating out of your hand. Well, I'm not buying."

I couldn't see a way out of this by talking, so I went for the escape. I pulled out my earring fast enough to give my ear a painful tug. I was placing the circle of the earring inside the pendant when Damian closed the distance between us. He grabbed at my arm, trying to stop me. But the earring clicked into place.

An instant later, the world dissolved in white light.

My insides lurched like someone had turned my guts inside out. My consciousness was overwhelmed by light and colour, as well as a buzzing in my brain.

I've no idea how long it lasted. Probably only seconds, but there was no reference, no sense of body or mind, just the brightness. Then I was somewhere else. A grey room.

I collapsed on the ground, barely aware of Damian collapsing beside me. I felt like I was about to be sick, my guts seething inside me. Good thing I'd been too nervous to have breakfast. My lungs heaved for air like I'd been pulled from the bottom of the ocean and my whole body was covered in a chill sweat. My brain had stalled and it took some moments for me to be aware of anything but the uncomfortable sensations in my body. Then I was able to look around at a bare grey room and Damian lying on the floor, heaving beside me, the smell of which wasn't helping me keep control of my own stomach. I'm ashamed to admit it, but I felt a guilty pleasure at the sight of him vomiting down his shirt.

Sorry, Blaze, if you're reading this.

At the time there were more serious things to worry about. Where the hell were we?

Chapter 11

"Where the hell are we?" Damian's question echoed my thoughts. He'd stopped throwing up now, but he still looked pale and shaky, a faint sheen of sweat clamming his skin. He looked as bad as I felt.

"I have no idea."

The walls, floor, and ceiling were made of a smooth grey substance. It wasn't metal and it wasn't painted; it looked more like someone had moulded the entire room out of plastic. There was a sunken rectangle that was hopefully some kind of door, but there was no apparent way of opening it. My handbag was lying on the floor beside me. It had been on my shoulder when the teleport had grabbed us. I dove into it now, pulling out my phone. I wasn't hugely surprised to see that there wasn't a signal. I grabbed the mimic sheet instead, hoping it had better range. I scrawled a quick message: *Where the hell am I?* I added a few exclamation marks at the end.

"Stop lying," Damian said. "I saw you fiddling with that thing. You did this."

He gestured towards my necklace, which still had the earring pressed inside it. Theoretically it should be broadcasting my distress signal to Nuke and the others. I just didn't have any way of knowing if it was working.

"This wasn't what I was expecting to happen," I said.

Damian laughed, "Looks like your armoured friends screwed you."

I'd been wondering that. Either the teleporter had somehow messed up or Navy had deliberately screwed me over and dumped me in this box.

On the floor beside me, the mimic sheet wiped clean. Damian noticed the change as well. As we watched, words edged themselves across the surface in Navy's neat handwriting. *That's a really good question.*

"What is that?" Damian asked. "Some kind of alien IM?"

"Pretty much."

I hauled myself to my feet. My legs still felt shaky but I made it to the rectangle that I hoped was the door and grabbed onto the wall for balance until the dizziness faded. Now that I was upright, I was aware of the dimensions of the room being off. The ceiling was higher than I would have expected, the door taller than would seem proportionate. It was a subtle thing, but jarring nonetheless. I poked around the door, looking for switches or sensors that would get it to open, but there was nothing but the blank, plasticky wall.

"Are you still signalling?" Damian asked. I turned to him, confused, and saw he was reading the question off the mimic sheet. I felt for the necklace, the earring was still pressed into place.

"Assuming the transmitter is working," I said.

Damian picked up the stylus and wrote down my answer. I was slightly surprised that he did so, but I guessed he wanted to get out of there as much as I did. It might have been a mistake for him to write the response because clearly his handwriting was a giveaway. The next message from Navy was an abrupt question: *Who is this?*

I returned to the floor beside Damian, since prodding the door was obviously not doing anything. I took back the stylus and gave a very quick summary of Damian confronting me and how he'd got caught up in the teleport event.

There was a significant pause before the reply came. I could only imagine what sort of discussions must have been taking place at the other end of this chat. The message came at last: *Do you trust him?*

I wrote back quickly: *Not in the slightest.*

"Hey!" protested Damian, who'd been reading over my shoulder. "I'm not the one who's been lying and sneaking about and collaborating with aliens."

"Navy's not an alien," I said quickly.

"Well what the hell kind of name is Navy for a human?"

"A codename, idiot."

Damian was glaring at me across the floor of our little plastic cell, "Look, love, I don't have to take this from some deceitful little girl who's up to her neck in this mess."

"Little girl?" If I hadn't felt that fainting or vomiting were still on the cards, I might have smacked him across his pompous face. Instead, we restricted ourselves to glaring. I don't know what might have happened if we'd been left alone in that little room for much longer with only each other's company. It probably wouldn't have been pretty.

Fortunately, our captors decided to show themselves. The door slid out and up. I hastily shoved the mimic sheet and stylus into my handbag just before two people walked in. They looked human enough, though taller than the norm and noticeably pale, but were dressed in silvery uniforms that I knew I'd seen before. These were some of the same people who'd attacked Ethan and I, who'd held Princess hostage during the fight at the Tower. The same as the man I'd killed.

Damian forced himself upright, standing before them and glaring up at them with as much force as had been recently directed towards me.

"Kidnapping us is a criminal act," he said, "and will not be tolerated." It might have been more impressive if he hadn't had vomit splatters down his tie, but still I had to give him credit for trying. The silver people didn't seem to care. They ignored him outright and turned to me.

"We want nameless traitor," one said.

"The what?"

"Traitor," he repeated. "You call… Nuke."

Traitor? I filed that description away with the hoard of suspicions I was keeping about Nuke but tried to keep my face blank.

"Lots of people are looking for him," I said.

"You lie to the Grey Lady," he said. "We know you serve him. Where is he?"

There was something strange about the way they were talking, with odd pauses in the middle of sentences, as though hunting for the right words. It took me a moment to figure it out. If I dredged up the remnants of knowledge from my GCSE German, I'd probably talk in the same way, all simple sentences and hesitations. These guys might be speaking English, but they weren't fluent in it. Which raised the question as to what language they would be fluent in.

"I don't know," I said.

"You lie," he said again. "You pretend to work for the Grey Lady, but you work for him."

I caught Damian glaring in my direction again but ignored him, "Why would you think that?"

"She asked us watch you. You talk to traitor."

So these guys were the ones who'd been spying on me, the ones Nuke's team had warned me about. Given their demonstration of teleporting technology, all that sneaking about at Megan's had presumably been for nothing. They must have known we'd been disappearing to see Nuke. The only good thing was that they apparently couldn't track the teleportation or they wouldn't need to question me.

Beside me, it was clear Damian's mind had been working rapidly too.

"You work for Mrs Grey?" he asked the silver guys. They looked at him. It was difficult to read their expressions, but disdain was the best approximation.

"We want traitor," one said. "She wants him not here. Now, we work with her. Later, not."

Damian was clearly struggling with the whole concept of Mrs Grey working with aliens. The aliens themselves didn't seem to care. They were still more interested in me.

"Where is traitor?" one asked. It was hard to separate them. They looked similar and there was nothing to distinguish their uniforms.

"I don't know." I figured the truth couldn't hurt. "He never told me."

"You met with him."

"That doesn't mean I knew where we were. He teleported me there and back again."

"You can talk to him."

I was holding my handbag, aware of the mimic sheet within it. It took all my resolve not to tighten my grip on it. My necklace was presumably still sending out its signal, no doubt they could pick that signal up.

"Why do you want him?" I asked.

The two aliens exchanged a look that I couldn't interpret.

"Pain," one answered. I wasn't quite sure how to interpret this either except that it probably wasn't good news for Nuke.

"Why should I help you?" I asked, desperately hoping that their answer wouldn't be the same as for the previous question. I was struggling to stay calm.

One of the aliens stepped up in front of me, looking down at me from a distance that was a little too close. I had to fight not to back away.

"We get traitor, you live," he said. "We not get traitor, you not. Tell him."

The aliens turned to the door, which opened for them without any apparent signal or interaction. They stepped out into a grey corridor.

Damian tried to charge after them. One turned, grabbing Damian before he could get more than a step outside. The alien buried a fist into Damian's gut and dumped him back inside the room. The door slid closed again with Damian on his knees inside the cell. He looked like he might throw up again.

"Worth a try," I commented. He shot me a withering look.

I pulled out the mimic sheet, which was now asking me what was happening. It was impressive how his neat handwriting still managed to convey worry. I quickly scribbled a summary of the conversation that had just happened. I hesitated before writing the word 'traitor', but included it anyway. There was another long pause before a reply.

"Are your friends going to rescue us?" Damian asked. "Or will they let these people kill us?"

I wished I had an answer for him. I wanted to believe that Nuke was mustering the cavalry to ride to our rescue, but I didn't know him well enough to be confident of it. The drawn out stillness of the mimic sheet wasn't helping my nerves.

Chapter 12

I had things other than the mimic sheet in my handbag. I wasn't expecting my wallet or purse to be particularly helpful, but I had the gun that Nuke had sent to me. I wasn't sure if the silver guys knew about this but figured they wouldn't have been so casual about walking into the cell with us if they did. I also wasn't sure about revealing it to Damian.

Partly it was because I didn't trust him, but partly it was because the silver guys were likely to be watching me. I'd spent the past few weeks assuming my every move was being monitored and I wasn't about to stop now. So I considered various plans in silence. As plans go, they were fairly primitive. I had one gun, an ally I couldn't be certain of and an entirely unknown situation on the other side of the door. Using the gun to cut myself out of the cell was a possibility, but one that would probably use up all the gun's power. I didn't have my armour to recharge it and I didn't plan on walking around enemy territory unarmed.

So that left me with plan B. I'd wait until the silver guys came back to talk to us again and then I'd shoot them. At least I could make certain of the power settings on the gun this time.

I paced the tiny cell. I wanted to be on my feet the next time the door opened and I had no way of knowing how long that would be. They could leave us in here for minutes, hours or days.

"So these guys work with Mrs Grey," said Damian.

"Yep."

"And they're aliens."

"Yep." Dealing with Mr Bleeding Obvious wasn't helping my nerves at all. I dug into my handbag again to check the mimic sheet. It was still blank.

"Maybe they're good aliens," he said, "and they're providing information to help us fight off the bad ones."

Despite my dislike for Damian, I knew what was going on in his head. He was trying to rationalise the situation to make it so that he hadn't been working for the bad guys. His perspective on the world had been turned on its head and he was trying to restructure it around him in such a way that he'd still come out a hero. It was exactly what I'd done when I realised I'd helped Ethan to be captured. I stopped pacing and looked at him.

"The last thing Professor Swinson ever did was to call me," I said. "He'd found something out about what Mrs Grey was planning and he warned me that it couldn't be allowed to happen. But he was killed before he could tell me what it was. Someone inside Grey's Tower murdered him. Someone who works for Mrs Grey."

"Do you know who?"

I shook my head, "If I knew that, I'd have made them pay for it."

"But you did know that Mrs Grey was collaborating with aliens?"

"Yeah, I knew that. Look, Damian, you had every reason not to trust me and you were right, I was trying to spy on Grey's Tower. But that doesn't make me the bad guy here. If we're going to get through this, we've got to focus on fighting them, not each other. Truce?"

I offered my hand. Damian hesitated a long time before taking it.

"Truce," he agreed. "But I still think you're a deceitful brat."

I smiled across our clasped hands, "And I think you're a pompous Neanderthal, so we're even."

Our hands parted and I reached into my handbag again for the mimic sheet. Still blank. I shifted the contents to make sure that I could grab the gun in a heartbeat if I needed to.

"Got any food in there, love?" Damian asked. I pulled out a pack of chewing gum from a side pocket and tossed it to him.

"Close enough," he said, putting a piece in his mouth and tossing it back. "Anything else?"

I still wasn't ready to show him the gun, but I pulled out my house keys. Attached to the key ring was a tiny pocket knife. Its blade was less than two inches long and blunt as hell, but it was *something*. I unclipped it from my keys and handed it over. Damian unfolded the blade and stared at it, looking like he might start laughing any moment.

"If you're going to get abducted by aliens," I said, "make sure you've got your handbag with you."

He did laugh then, the first moment of humour we shared.

"I'm not sure it would go with my shoes," he said.

***

It must have been at least an hour before I got a message on the mimic sheet. There was no reference to my previous communication, no indication of what Nuke planned to do about the ultimatum. There was just a simple statement in Navy's neat writing: *You're in orbit. Can't get a stable fix and you're moving too fast to teleport to you safely.*

I showed the message to Damian.

"So much for rescue," he muttered.

"I guess if we're getting out of here we're going to have to do it ourselves."

He looked at the pocket knife and muttered, "Great."

We both paced a little more, which required cautious timing so that we didn't collide mid-cell.

"We've got to take them by surprise when they next come in," Damian started to plan.

I'd been thinking along the same lines, but I cut him off, "These guys have been spying on me for weeks. Do you honestly think they'd leave us in this cell and not be watching us?"

Damian looked around our bare, grey cell, "I don't see any hidden cameras."

"Just rewind that last sentence and try to turn your brain on this time."

"Fine. So what you're saying, sweetheart, is that we can't discuss how we're going to get out of this mess?"

"Not unless you can think of a way for us to do so without them hearing everything we plan and being prepared for it."

There was a drawn-out silence and then Damian grinned, "Igpay atinlay?"

I laughed, "Atthay ightmay orkway."

Given their apparent lack of familiarity with the English language, using pig Latin seemed a good bet to throw them off the scent. I'll admit it wasn't exactly masterful cryptography, but we were improvising. We communicated slowly in our makeshift code, coming up with a fairly basic plan. As we talked, I kept checking the mimic sheet, hoping for something from Navy. At last, a message appeared saying they were going to test teleporting. *Stand somewhere with space around you,* the message read.

So I stood in the middle of the cell while Damian stepped back to give a bit more room. There came a bright glow in the air a little to my side, solidifying into a small shape that hung there for a moment. As soon as the light vanished, it fell and I reached out to catch it.

It was a Rubik's Cube. At least, it had been. It was distorted, stretched out so that is was now twice as wide as it should be, bent to a slight curve as well. It was as though some powerful hand had grabbed hold of either side of it and stretched. One of the little coloured squares fell from it, shattering when it hit the floor, made remarkably brittle by the distortions.

"I'd rather they didn't try that with me," Damian said.

I agreed. If these sort of distortions were possible with a lump of plastic, I didn't want to think what might happen to a human being who tried this. I quickly got out the mimic sheet and described to Navy what had happened.

I'd barely finished when our captors returned. I guess they'd picked up the energy of Navy's teleportation and wanted to make sure we weren't escaping.

The door opened and Damian charged at the first alien in view, the little pocket knife clutched in his hand as he thrust. I had the gun out of my handbag. While the first alien defended against Damian's attack, he twisted round and I had a clear shot of exposed back.

I fired and saw the light of my attack shimmer harmlessly across the silvery surface of his uniform. The only effect of the gun was to draw attention towards me. As the man turned, I raised the gun and fired a blast of energy directly into his face. This time, the stunner worked and the guy crumpled to the ground in front of me.

The second alien was ignoring Damian to charge at me, the cell door closing behind me.

"The door!" I yelled at Damian.

The silver guy made a grab for the gun, seizing my right arm round the wrist. I twisted my arm in an attempt to break his grip. I put my left hand on his arm to give me leverage while I tried to manoeuvre behind him, out of reach of his other arm.

His fingers were digging painfully into my tendons and the gun toppled out of my useless grasp.

My arms were entirely occupied, so I had to use legs. I dealt a sharp kick on the back of his calf. As he stumbled, his grip on my arm loosened enough that I could twist it free. We stood apart for a moment.

He dove for the gun. I went for the option of kicking him in the face instead. He rolled backwards, purplish blood streaming from his nose and I kicked again. As he tried to find his feet, I dropped into a crouch, seized up the gun and fired a shot into his bleeding face.

He was dodging sideways at the time so the shot barely grazed him, but it was enough for him to look momentarily dazed and then let me get the direct shot.

"Um... Jenny!"

Damian was in the doorway, trying to hold it open. The door was partly closed and Damian was clearly using all his strength to stop it shutting completely, his back braced against the frame, foot and hands pressed against the door's edge. I grabbed my fallen handbag and ducked under his arms, squeezing myself through the gap between him and the door. He slid out behind me and the door slammed shut.

We stood together in a grey corridor of the same substance as the cell. He glared at me while he rubbed some life back into his arms.

"How come you didn't tell me you had that?" he nodded to the gun.

"I didn't want them to know."

He couldn't easily argue with that point, but he could glare at me for it.

I was concerned about the gun. It seemed their silvery-grey uniforms had similar properties to the outer layer of Nuke and co's armour, in that it deflected the energy of my weapon. I knew that if I dialled up the power, it could cut through, but I wasn't about to start killing people. That meant if I wanted to knock them out, I had to get a headshot. In a cramped cell when we were standing a few feet apart, that was one thing. I wasn't sure I'd manage it so easily out here if we got into a fire fight. I was also acutely aware of how vulnerable we were.

The corridor was short, maybe thirty metres long, with three doors on either side and one at the far end. At least the doors had obvious controls on this side. We couldn't stand in the corridor waiting to be caught, so I readied my gun while Damian triggered one of the nearest doors.

It led to cramped sleeping quarters. There were narrow bunks in stacks of three on either side of us, with storage compartments on the far wall and some strange gear standing on a waist-high shelf. Probably their equivalent of a hairdryer or something, but I wasn't about to start pressing buttons at random to figure it out. Everything was grey and utilitarian and built to cram into as tight a space as possible.

"So we can expect at least four more of these guys," Damian said.

"Assuming that they've got a full complement," I said. Possibly they were down to three, given that one of their number had been killed, but I wasn't going to say that.

"Come on," Damian said, but I ignored him and went to the storage cupboards. "Are you going to rifle through their stuff?" he asked.

That was exactly what I was doing, pulling out a couple of their tunic-type uniforms made of the shimmering silver-grey fabric. I tossed one to Damian and started hauling the other over my head.

"I doubt that's going to disguise us," he said.

"This fabric deflected the energy of my attack," I said. "That means there's a reasonable chance it would do the same with their weapons. It's worth a shot."

Damian shrugged and pulled on his new outfit. They were hardly flattering and they certainly hadn't been designed for a female body, but they stretched well enough to fit and I would be grateful for any protection they might provide.

Then we headed back into the corridor to try door number two.

Chapter 13

We never made it as far as door number two. When we got back out into the corridor, the door at the other end opened, and in came another pair of silver-uniformed people. These ones were better armed, carrying guns about the size of rifles. The first blast of energy exploded against the corridor wall as Damian shoved me aside. We ended up back inside the living quarters and Damian jabbed the button to close the door behind us. Unfortunately, the door controls only seemed to have "open" and "close", with no concept of "lock".

"Any bright ideas, sweetheart?" Damian asked. He kept his finger jammed against the "close'" button in the hope that might override whatever might be done by the guys outside.

Unfortunately, I was all out of bright ideas. I grabbed the mimic sheet out of my handbag and crawled a quick message: *Help!* There was nothing else on me that might be useful; I wasn't about to MacGyver an escape hatch with a tube of concealer and lip gloss.

The door started to open, despite Damian's frantic button-pushing.

"Drop!" I yelled, and started firing my gun at around head-height for the aliens. They dodged out of the way, putting the wall between my attacks and them. Damian had been crouching beside the open door and now he leapt out, tackling the legs of one of the aliens. The two ended up on the floor in a tangled mess of limbs, the rifle clattering down beside them. The other alien fired at Damian, who screamed in pain despite the protection offered by the silver uniform, which sent the energy shimmering across its surface.

In the brief struggle, the standing alien had moved into the doorway again, giving me a line of sight. I fired my gun rapidly, hitting the man's head on the third attempt. He crumpled. I moved out into the corridor, aiming my gun at the head of the other one. He was still sprawled on the floor, having detangled himself for Damian. I kept my eyes on the alien, noting from Damian's wheezing breath that he was at least still alive.

"How many of you are there?" I asked.

I had no idea if the guy understood me. His mouth peeled back in an inhuman snarl.

He made a dive for his fallen rifle. I fired my gun, but didn't manage a clean hit until after he'd pressed a button on the rifle's side. A whirring noise began to build in a crescendo from somewhere inside the weapon. I couldn't be sure what it was, but it didn't sound promising.

I grabbed Damian and put an arm around his back to help him up. He was clenching down on a cry of pain as we hurried back into the living quarters. I lowered him down onto the nearest bunk and went back only long enough to grab the other rifle, the one that wasn't screeching horrendously. I slammed down on the "close" button just in time.

The explosion was deafening. The force reverberated around us. The door buckled inwards, the plasticky material striking me with enough strength to knock me down, and a wave of heat and light washed over me.

It was over in moments. I picked myself gingerly off the floor. I would be bruised as hell, but everything seemed to be in working order. I wasn't sure Damian was so lucky. He was sitting on the bunk, pain flooding his face with every breath. He lowered his hands from his ears and looked at me, before turning to look at the warped mess that had once been the door.

"Some people are sore losers," he said.

"Some people are sore winners," I commented. "Let me look."

I went over to him, lifting away the ruined mess of silvery material. Below it, charred fabric clung to charred flesh; his shirt and jacket had been burned through in patches. His back was a mess of burns, radiating out from the point of impact. Angry red skin was already blistering, even away from the main wound, tendrils of burn spreading around his sides, even onto his chest and stomach. The uniform must have spread the energy across his body, carrying the pain across a wider area. I suggested as much to Damian.

"So much for your theory about the shirts being good protection," he hissed as I peeled off what was left of his shirt where it was clinging to the blisters.

"If all this energy had been concentrated in one place," I said, "you'd be dead."

"Well, we might not have long to wait for that anyway."

I would have said something encouraging at that point, but I'd actually been worrying along similar lines. I didn't have anything in my handbag that could treat infections or sterilise the wounds. I wasn't sure what his long-term odds would be without something like that. In the short term, there was no way he'd be able to do much fighting. I remembered how painful my burns had been after the boat incident, and those had been relatively minor. Plus I had been pumped up on major painkillers after my injuries.

That sparked a thought. I rummaged in my handbag and pulled out a small pack of ibuprofen.

"How much stuff do you have in there?" Damian sounded astonished.

"Anything I think might be useful," I answered. I generally carried a little packet of painkillers in my bag so that I'd have them handy when cramps hit. I wasn't sure how helpful they'd be in dulling the pain from the sort of injuries Damian had, but they had to be better than nothing.

While he swallowed the pills, I inspected the rifle. It had a series of buttons on its side that were of unknown function. After seeing the self-destruct button in action, I wasn't about to start experimenting. The other side had power settings that were similar to the controls on my handgun. Remarkably similar. If we got out of this alive, I'd have to have a word with Nuke about this.

I hesitated over the weapons for a moment. I couldn't use both of them at once. I was much more familiar with the handgun, but the rifle was obviously more powerful. Given the lack of effect my little gun had through their uniform, the sensible option was for me to keep the rifle. From the state of Damian, I knew it worked through their defences. Even so, I dialled the power levels down slightly. I didn't want more deaths on my conscience.

I offered the handgun to Damian. He took it reluctantly.

"I've never really fired a gun before," he said.

"Then just keep pulling the trigger until you hit something," I advised.

"How did you get so good?"

"I was junior laser tag champion for north-west England."

He blinked a few times, "Laser tag?"

"Don't knock it."

The principles were surprisingly similar, since these guns didn't have projectiles. I didn't have to worry about recoil or conservation of momentum. I could just aim and fire. The only big difference was that I'd never been terrified for my life during laser tag tournaments.

With guns sorted, I suggested finding a new shirt for Damian in the storage compartments, but he shook his head. He wasn't sure he could cope with anything over the burns and, if he took a second hit, he didn't think he was likely to survive it anyway. I didn't argue.

"Just stay behind me," I said.

We couldn't sit around in this room forever. Before we moved back out, I checked the mimic sheet again, reported that Damian was hurt and asked what they were planning. Different handwriting replied that Navy was trying to figure out how to teleport safely to us.

They'd said we were in orbit, so I guessed that meant we were moving very fast relative to the teleporter, even if it didn't feel like it from our perspective. Navy was used to using the teleporter to points that were in a fixed position relative to the starting place. I wanted him to get it right first, because if he was planning on teleporting us off, I didn't want to end up like the Rubik's Cube.

Damian stood stiffly, clutching my gun tightly. I walked over to what remained of the door. It must have taken a huge portion of the blast. Now there was a twisted wreck of half-melted plastic bent into the room. I didn't even try to open the door, just climbed out through the gap left by the destruction. I offered a hand to help Damian through, but he ignored the gesture and climbed through on his own.

The short corridor was a mess. Charred burn marks decorated the walls. The two bodies were little more than charcoal on the floor with a smell of burnt meat. The door across from the living quarters was in nearly as bad a state, bent from its frame by the force of the blast. As part of our exploration, I pressed the button to open it, but the door was jammed. It tried to slide aside, shook slightly and then gave up. There was no way it was going to work after the damage. I peered through the small hole that now existed between door and frame. I could make out little of the room beyond, but there didn't appear to be anyone in there.

The door leading to the cell wasn't quite as bad, but it was slightly warped out of its frame. Hopefully that would help with keeping the other two contained once they regained consciousness. Further down the corridor, though they were blackened from the explosion, the other doors seemed to be intact.

I led the way to the next one, aiming the rifle inside before pressing the button. It was some kind of kitchen. At least, that was the best guess we had and obviously these guys needed to eat something. There were more storage compartments with packets of stuff that neither of us was going to attempt to eat, however hungry we might have been. We didn't dare press buttons on the thing that looked a bit like a microwave, set into the wall. There were no people in there and so we moved on quickly.

Behind the next door was a room with a couple of chairs and machinery we didn't dare breathe too closely to in case we accidentally crashed whatever we were in. It was all glittering lights and screens of shifting colour with symbols and weird alien icons fading in and out of view. This could have been their cockpit, the equipment they used for spying on me, or their entertainment centre, for all we knew. Whatever it was, we backed out of there in a hurry and closed the door.

Back in the hallway, there were still more doors. We tried two more without finding anything particularly useful. One might have been a lab, the other resembled a lounge except with sturdy safety harnesses on all the seats. Then there was just one left: the door at the opposite end to the cell, through which the enemy had earlier come. Weapons ready, mindful that there might be more crew around, we went over and I pressed the button to activate the door.

The empty room beyond was something of an anti-climax. It was a tiny space, barely big enough for both of us to go in at once, with no furniture, equipment or anything else to indicate what the two crew members had been doing in there.

Then I looked up.

The little room didn't have a ceiling, just a tall shaft reaching up like a grey chimney. There was a ladder stretching up into the darkness, the first rungs starting a little above my head. The ship, or whatever we were on, continued up that way.

"I won't be able to make it up there," said Damian, looking at the ladder. Even I was frustrated that these aliens didn't start their ladder at ground level. There was no way in hell I was going to be able to climb onto it holding the rifle, so I exchanged weapons with Damian again.

"Keep an eye on our friends," I nodded towards the cell door. He agreed. I tucked the small handgun into my handbag and adjusted the strap over my shoulder so it wouldn't slip off mid-climb. Then it was time to tackle the ladder.

I jumped, grabbing hold of a rung a couple from the bottom. Dangling off the ladder, legs flailing, I managed to pull myself up and grab the rung above, hauling my body up again. My arms were burning with the effort to get myself high enough that I could get my feet onto the lowest rung. I made it, though, and leaned into the ladder for a few moments to get my breath back and get some feeling back into my hands.

Then I started to climb. I'm not sure how long the shaft was, maybe a couple of hundred metres. Strangely, the climb seemed to get easier as I went. It look less and less effort to lift my body to the next rung of the ladder and soon I was almost floating along, pushing off against the rungs to give me momentum. I think that was the first moment that I really began to believe, at a subconscious level, the statements about being in orbit.

Then I emerged from the top of the shaft and any doubts I had vanished in the face of the sight that lay before me.

Chapter 14

No experience in my life, before or since, has been as awe-inspiring as the moment I emerged into the navigation capsule and saw the Earth below me. An entire wall of the circular capsule was made of a transparent substance that gave me a perfect view of the planet below.

I couldn't really make out continents or countries, just a mass of hazy blue mixed in with patches of brown and green, all iced with a fluffy layer of clouds. It hung in front of me like a jewel, filling the window with majestic serenity. As I floated before that window, I felt like I could reach out and touch it.

Everything that had happened to me, all the painful and terrifying things, were worth it for that view.

I don't know how long I stared. It must have been at least a minute. Then I pulled myself away from the spectacle outside and paid attention to where I was. This capsule was almost certainly the pilot's area. There was a padded chair complete with safety harnesses, positioned facing the giant window. On either side of the chair, panels of switches and displays were set to swivel into place for the pilot to operate. There was very little else, just the entrances to the shafts, for there was a second one opposite the one I'd come through.

The shafts were spinning around this little capsule. Or perhaps the capsule was spinning and the shafts were still. Or both. Whichever I was in seemed the stable one, altering my perspective enough to make me feel dizzy. Either way, it was like the capsule had a metal band around it that was constantly spinning, and attached to that band were the tunnels down to the rest of the ship.

I positioned myself at the entrance to one and tried to figure out if it was the one I'd climbed up. From here, they seemed identical and I'd been so distracted by the view that, with all the spinning, I wasn't sure which was which. Fortunately, I caught a glimpse of Damian all the way along one of them, so I knew to choose the other. I pushed off from the edge of the room and began floating feet-first along the other one.

I kept my hands on the ladder so that, as I felt the effects of pseudo-gravity reasserting themselves, I could get my limbs onto the rungs and climb down the rest of the way. At the bottom of the ladder I had the reverse issue to the one I'd had getting up and lowered myself by my arms for a couple of rungs before letting go and dropping the rest of the way.

I ended up in a little, bare compartment that was the mirror of the one which Damian waited in. The ground felt stable beneath my feet. Hard to believe that I'd flipped a hundred and eighty degrees from somewhere that felt equally stable a few hundred metres above me. I wanted to laugh at the surreal nature of the experience.

But there was half a rotating spaceship to explore. I pulled my gun from my handbag and pressed the open button beside the door.

Something smacked me in the face.

What followed undoubtedly qualifies as the most embarrassing fight of my existence, but I promised Navy that I'd keep these accounts as accurate as memory allows.

While I was reeling and dazed from the first blow, my attacker whacked me in the stomach with the same something which had earlier hit me in the face. I can only assume it was the alien spaceship equivalent of the lead piping. I was gasping for breath as my torso exploded in pain when I was hit again, this time the blow catching my arm, which I'd instinctively brought in across my stomach as a reaction to the previous blow. Tingling pain flowed down to my fingers and I dropped the damn gun.

My attacker reached out with a foot to kick the gun behind him, leaving me unarmed in that little cupboard-room. I managed to straighten up and get my first good look at my attacker. He was like the others on this ship, human-looking and wearing the same silvery-grey uniform. What was different about this guy was the expression of terror on his face. He held up a long piece of grey tubing, clutching it like it was a particularly blunt sword. He would have looked pretty pathetic if it wasn't for the fact that I was hurt and he was armed. Sort of.

"Relax," I said, holding out a hand in a calming gesture. "I'm sure we can talk this through."

I'm confident that he didn't understand a word I said. To be fair, I didn't have a clue what he said back to me. It sounded like a string of clicks and vowel sounds. We stood there for a moment, staring at each other in confusion.

I shifted slightly, trying to slip my handbag down my shoulder slightly, thinking I could swing it into the tubing and get this on an even footing. The man noticed the movement and took a fraction of a step back. He was clutching onto the tubing so tightly I'm surprised he didn't leave finger marks.

A bright point of light caught my eye. In the corridor behind the guy, a patch of air smaller than my fist glowed with teleportation energy as something small and metal materialised. As it appeared, it seemed to move slightly sideways. It clunked into the wall and then tumbled down to the floor with a clink of metal.

Tube guy glanced round at the noise and that was my moment. I stepped forward, swinging my handbag into the tube to get both objects out of the way. I closed the gap with a punch to the solar plexus. As he stumbled backwards, it was a simple matter to hook my leg behind his as I threw him further off balance with a second punch. He flailed backwards, tripping over my foot and his own and ending up in an ungainly heap on the floor. I actually felt bad for the guy for a moment.

Then he grabbed my gun, which he'd managed to land on, and he started shooting at me.

There was no cover and the first shot the man fired missed me by a mile but hit the door button and I couldn't get the damn thing to shut between us. Fortunately, the stolen uniform and the fact that he was a really lousy shot meant that I was fine. Light struck the front of the shirt and shimmered across the metallic surface. After about the sixth hit, I started to feel light-headed, sort of tingly.

I thought I was imagining the glow at first. But bright white light formed into a figure in black armour, standing behind the man who was shooting me. It was my Knight, coming to rescue me like every clichéd fairy tale I'd believed in when I was a little girl. He pulled the gun from its holster, aiming at the alien.

"Head shot," I called out.

Knight shifted his aim slightly and fired, hitting the guy in the head on his first shot. The alien fell unconscious, my gun falling on the floor beside him. I grabbed hold of the wall to stay upright, the effect of the energy weapon leaving me somewhat weakened.

Then Knight stepped over the unconscious man and wrapped his arms around me. Being hugged by someone in full armour is a really weird experience. There's no warmth, no feeling of human contact, but still I leant into his strength, all the fear of recent events fading away. The pain of the past few weeks, the loss and separation didn't seem to matter anymore. I just let him hold me.

"Yeah," Knight said. "Yes, I'm alive. I'm fine."

For a moment, I was confused. I blame it on the effects of being shot. A moment later, I realised he was probably talking to someone back on base using the communicator built into his helmet.

"You don't have to sound so surprised that I'm alive," Knight said.

"You didn't see the Rubik's Cube," I said.

There came another bright light followed by a materialising figure in black armour. This time it was Princess, and she held a very large duffel bag in her arms.

"Got you a present," she said. Knight and I parted. I nearly tripped over the unconscious man to do so. I took the bag from Princess setting it on the floor to open it up. Inside were several large, bulky black objects. She'd brought my Omega armour.

"Why didn't Knight bring this?" I asked.

"Because we weren't sure he'd get here in one piece," she said. "We can replace Knight, but your armour is unique."

"Thanks," Knight said, laughing at her teasing, but I felt a note of honesty behind the comments. Knight hadn't been sure he'd get here intact, after the problems they'd had with the first experiments teleporting up here. Even with Navy figuring out the issues, through experimenting on inanimate objects, this had been a major risk for Knight to take.

That realisation brought with it an overwhelming sense of emotion. If it hadn't been for the dangerous situation, I might have burst into tears or ripped his helmet off to kiss him or I don't know what. Instead, I tried to maintain my composure as I pulled out the pieces of my Omega armour and started to put them on.

That armour is made of large pieces that clip together, so it's supposed to be easy to put on in a hurry. If you've ever tried to get dressed when you're in a rush, you'll know what it's like when your figures fumble everything. Getting that armour on in that corridor seemed to have become a ridiculously difficult challenge. I fumbled with clasps and got my foot caught in one of the leg pieces. Princess stepped in to help me out, probably because the spectacle of me struggling to get dressed was too embarrassing to watch.

I had to suck in my stomach in order to clasp the torso piece closed. Over the last few weeks, I'd had to cut out my usual exercise while my lungs healed and I guessed that evenings eating takeaways in my rented room hadn't done my physique any favours. But there would be time to worry about that later.

Right now, we had to deal with the unconscious alien on the floor; the two in the cell; Damian injured, somewhere on the other half of the spaceship; as well as the teleport light of Nuke arriving to join us.

I slipped my earpiece in and was fastening shut my helmet when I heard a stream of swearing coming over the communications lines.

"Navy, what's happened?" asked Nuke.

There came more swearing and then Navy answered, "The targeting controls. They've blown."

"How long until you can fix it?" asked Princess.

"I don't think you understand me. They've blown. There is smoke pouring out of the teleporter. I think I fried the circuits trying to lock onto a moving target. I can't fix this."

"So we're stuck here?" she asked.

"These guys have teleportation technology," I said. "Possibly better than yours." At least, I was assuming it was better, since they'd managed to hijack Navy's signal and get me here in the first place.

"I think you'd better show me the controls," said Nuke.

I agreed, but suggested we check out this half of the ship first. From our brief investigation, it seemed that this half was doing all the work. Engines, life support, and half a dozen other vital components were apparently behind the walls of the corridor. At least, according to Nuke. I wasn't entirely sure how he could identify them so easily, and after all the comments earlier about traitors, I longed to get somewhere less life-threatening so I could demand some straight answers out of him.

As it was, Nuke declared that while the machinery was over here, the controls that drove them must all be on the other half of the ship.

"Why the hell would someone design a spaceship in two pieces?" asked Princess.

The answer came via the earpiece from Navy. "Artificial gravity. The larger the radius, the slower the rotation required in order to simulate the same level of gravity through centripetal forces. It also reduces the disorientation that would occur with smaller radii where your head would be experiencing slightly different gravitational effects to your feet. By building the ship with two connected pieces, it has a lot less mass than if they had built a solid ship big enough to create artificial gravity without ill-effects."

I wished I could see the faces of my companions to see if they'd followed Navy's explanation better than I had.

"Even so," said Princess, "why not put the controls near the systems they're controlling?"

"Probably so that the crew could spend most of their time in one half of the ship," said Nuke. "All they would need to live and do their jobs is over on the other half and they only need to come into this half to perform maintenance, or when escaped prisoners are going around shooting at them."

"He shot at me." I gestured at the unconscious body. I felt strangely defensive after Nuke's comment. He just chuckled.

"Let's go over to the other side," he said.

Knight had a final question, "What should we do about him?"

He gestured at the unconscious crew member. Nuke clapped Knight on the shoulder.

"Thanks for volunteering for guard duty," Nuke said. He headed to the ladder. Knight looked at Princess. Even with his mask hiding his expression, he didn't need to ask.

"Fine," she said. "I'll stand guard."

I was glad of my mask which hid my expression, because I was sure I was blushing furiously. Knight wanted to stay with me. OK, it was hideously outdated if he wanted to protect me. But it was still sweet. Or maybe he was just afraid to let me out of his sight after fearing he'd lost me to these aliens. Or maybe he'd just missed me. Whatever his reasoning, I was thrilled that he wanted to stay near me.

I retrieved the fallen handgun and put it into the holster of my armour. Then I picked up my handbag and slung it over my shoulder, which earned me a chuckle from Knight. I realised that I must have looked ridiculous in my full Omega gear with my handbag over my shoulder, but I wasn't about to leave my bag behind. Besides, it had been incredibly useful. I ignored Knight's laughter and headed to the ladder and the other half of the ship.

Chapter 15

We climbed up the ladder together, Nuke leading the way. Knight had offered me a leg-up to get onto the lower rungs. I gratefully accepted the help because my arms were still sore from the earlier climb, along with my skirmish in the corridor. Besides, light though the armour was, I was carrying extra weight now. I heard Knight ask Princess for a leg-up as well and tried not to be jealous. He was just being practical after all. I focused on the climb.

When we reached the rotating capsule in the middle, Nuke was inspecting the controls around the seat, almost oblivious to the view outside. Knight's reaction was much more like mine. He held onto the top of the ladder he'd just climbed and hung in the air, staring out at the globe in front of us. Swirls of white cloud decorated the atmosphere, but we could make out patches of blue and green below.

"Whoa!" Knight murmured. "This is... wow."

I chuckled behind my helmet, joining him in wonder. "That sums it up."

Knight glanced towards Nuke, who was holding himself steady on the back of the chair and carefully looking at the controls in turn.

"You've got no soul," Knight commented.

"I'm busy," he said.

"Come on," I said to Knight, leading the way down the other ladder. At the end, I dropped down into the little room to be met by Damian, who was aiming the rifle at me with wide-eyed fear.

"It's me," I said.

"Jenny?"

"Omega," I corrected. "We use codenames only when we're wearing armour." I stood out of the way for Knight to drop down and introduced him by his codename to Damian.

"So, you're wandering around alien spaceships with topless guys?" said Knight. "Should I be jealous?"

I gave a snort of laughter. Damian looked somewhat offended by my reaction.

"Are they our rescue party?" Damian asked, a cynical tone to his voice.

"Sort of," I answered, and explained about the teleporter issues. Above us, Nuke was making his way down the ladder. Hopefully he would put his mysterious knowledge to good use and tell us that he could send us all back safely. While we waited, Damian was looking curiously back and forth between Knight and I.

"Why is your armour different?" he asked.

I saw no point in lying. "Because Professor Swinson made mine."

By now, Nuke joined us and I quickly explained the layout of the ship, indicating the rooms in turn. He went into the room that had all the shiny equipment. He appeared to know what he was doing, because he started pressing some of the buttons and looking at the readouts that appeared on screens among all the flickering lights. I was standing in the doorway so I didn't have a clear view of the screens, but what I could see didn't look remotely like English.

It is largely because of his confident behaviour on that ship that I now base my belief that Nuke wasn't human. I know that might not seem like much evidence, but when you combine it with all the little anomalies, is it really that hard to believe that he got his knowledge of alien technology because he was an alien? Navy and I have debated the subject many times, but I think the most important point is that we don't know for sure. If Nuke had ever really trusted us, we wouldn't need to debate it. Can you really blame me for not trusting him?

"Hmm," Nuke said. "There's been teleportation activity."

"Could it have picked up our arrival?" Knight asked.

"No, this was triggered by the system." Nuke studied the screen some more, pressing another button. Then he left the room, pushing past me and Knight into the corridor. He went straight for the door at the end, the one leading into the cell. Nuke pressed the button to open the door without hesitation.

The cell was empty.

**

Clearly the two prisoners in the cell had some sort of remote control for the teleporter on the ship. And apparently they'd done something to lock us out of the controls. Either that or Nuke didn't understand their technology as well as he seemed to. He was debating what had happened with Navy over the phone, seeing if they could use what he could access of this ship's teleporter and connect it to what was still working of Navy's. The answer seemed to be "no". At least, not so that Navy would have any confidence of it working.

Given that Navy had done the seemingly impossible and got three people up here, I wasn't willing to try something he was actually declaring impossible.

That left us with just one option. We were in a ship, after all, and it had flight controls. Nuke was confident he could fly the ship, which just added to my suspicions when I remembered how long it had taken me to learn to drive, even with lessons. I wouldn't have dared attempt to parallel park a spaceship on the first attempt, so Nuke obviously knew more than he was letting us in on.

There were several problems that needed to be addressed, one of which was simply where to put it. We needed to bring the ship into land somewhere we could get back from, but remote enough not to be noticed. We couldn't exactly land a big rotating spaceship in the middle of York. Nuke and Navy were on the phone to each other, debating landing spots, while the rest of us handled our prisoner.

He came round under Princess's watchful eye and we managed, through the waving of guns and much pantomime, to get him to cross over between the two halves of the ship. Either he was a good actor or he really did have no idea what any of us were saying. Princess kept her gun aimed at him, but he seemed to have given up the fight.

While Nuke was setting up in the capsule, we were getting ready in the lounge area. There were just enough seats, each a padded armchair that was narrow enough that sitting down meant being pressed on either side by the cushioned sides, which must have been hell for Damian with his injuries. There were also multi-strand harnesses that fastened across chest and waist. These safety features actually worried me more than if this had just been a lounge. We each strapped in.

Knight was in the seat next to mine. He reached a hand over the high side of his chair towards me. I took it. Protective gloves stole away any sense of human contact, but I was grateful for it nonetheless.

That short flight had so many horrors that it's hard to say what was the worst part of it. There was the shaking, which rattled us all in our chairs and at times made it feel like the ship was about to rip apart at the seams. There was Nuke's voice in our ears, talking to Navy about the status of the flight, quoting speeds and altitudes that seemed far too high for any sane hope of survival. The occasional notes of panic in Nuke's voice didn't help at all. Then there was the roller-coaster lurching in my stomach as acceleration, gravity and the ship's spin fought with each other for dominance. Throwing up in my helmet seemed like a real possibility at times.

All I could do was cling on to Knight's hand, close my eyes, and wish desperately for this to be over.

I don't know how long that nightmarish flight took. Time stretched out and every moment seemed a lifetime. Then there came the moment when I heard Nuke mention landing thrusters.

The shaking was worse than ever. Knight's fingers were clenched around my own. Then there came a horrendous, screeching of metal and deafening crash, accompanied by a thump of impact that knocked the breath from my lungs for a moment.

And all was still.

For a moment, I wondered if I was dead. Then I opened my eyes.

I was lying back in my chair. Despite the layout of the room, down was very definitely behind me now, which gave us some interesting issues. In front of me, on the other side of the room, Princess and Damian were hanging from their harnesses.

Damian had passed out sometime during the flight, no doubt the pain of his injuries was more than his body could cope with during the violent motion. Standing on the wall of the room and getting him out of the chair was challenging. By the end of it, his wounds were oozing blood where the edges of the harness had been cutting in.

In the time it took to get Damian down, Nuke had figured out the escape hatch and come to find us.

"Bats and Valiant are on their way," Nuke said, "but it will take them a few hours to get here. I tried to put us somewhere remote, but someone's bound to have picked us up."

"We should get out of here," said Knight.

Nuke shook his head, "We can't let this technology get into the hands of Mrs Grey."

"We can't exactly hide a spaceship," Princess pointed out.

"No, but we can take what we can and destroy the rest."

I thought of how I'd felt when I'd seen the Earth from orbit. It seemed a crime to destroy something that could offer so beautiful a sight, but I could understand where Nuke was coming from. We'd destroyed the quantum inflector rather than let Mrs Grey put it to some nefarious use. Who knew what she might achieve if she had the power of this ship?

"We need to salvage what we can from the ship and then get out of here," Nuke said.

He issued us our orders. Knight and I were to take the unconscious Damian out of the ship. We were to find somewhere that gave us cover but let us see anyone approaching. We were to tend Damian and act as lookouts in case someone came to investigate the crash. Princess was given instructions on components to pull out of the teleporter while Nuke dealt with our prisoner. He took off his helmet and was removing his earpiece as I left the lounge area, so I've no idea what Nuke might have said to get the prisoner's cooperation. The fact that they were able to communicate at all was another layer to my suspicions against Nuke.

Knight and I manoeuvred Damian with difficulty along the tunnel to the capsule. We had to crawl, one pulling him, one pushing him, along what was now the tunnel's floor. We didn't want to scrape his injuries against the ground, so we took another of the silvery tunics and laid him on that, towing the cloth and carrying Damian on top of it. It was cramped, uncomfortable and awkward, but I couldn't easily complain when I knew that everything would be a thousand times worse for Damian, who was still out cold from the pain of his injuries.

The exit hatch was behind the pilot's seat in the capsule. Nuke had already forced it open so, each of us with an arm around Damian, we stepped out onto a landscape of rocks and grass and winter heather beneath a grey sky. Rain fell in a misty drizzle that reduced visibility, hopefully giving us a better chance of not having made the front page of every newspaper in the country. The ship had crashed into a shallow dip, where there was a slight rise in the ground on three sides.

Knight and I made our way up the nearest slope, feet sinking into heather and soggy ground, lumbering with Damian between us. At the top of the slope, we found a patch of heather and scrubby bushes. It wasn't much cover, but when Damian was lying down he was pretty well hidden, resting on the tunic so his wounds didn't get infected from the dirty ground. We could then sit among the bushes without being too obvious, looking down over slopes of grass and heather to distant fields, with a road and a small cluster of buildings situated in one direction. The ship looked bizarre, surrounded by wild ground, a strange contraption of blackened metal on ground faintly scorched by its landing. It had scarred a line of earth through the heather and half-buried itself in the base of the slope.

"Did we just crash a spaceship on the North York Moors?" I asked.

"Apparently," Knight answered.

"Why the hell does everything keep coming back to York?" I asked.

Navy must have been listening in, because he answered via the earpiece, "There aren't that many places you can land a spaceship without being seen by a few thousand people. At least, not places where we can rescue you from afterwards. We considered the Cairngorms, but that would have been trickier for Bats to reach you."

I looked at Damian beside us. He was still out cold, his face white beneath the sheen of falling rain. None of us could give him the attention he needed. I wondered if we should be keeping him dry or if the rain was a good thing. You were supposed to run cold water over burns after all. I wished I had enough medical knowledge to be sure one way or the other.

"How long until Bats gets here?" I asked.

"About four hours," Navy replied. "Maybe less if he breaks a few speed limits on the way."

So we waited. Knight and I sat facing opposite directions, looking out for any sign of danger or our allies. There wasn't much else to do. We couldn't even really talk, knowing that the others would be able to hear every word over the earpieces. So I could just think about all the things I would say to Ethan if we really were alone.

While we waited, Princess came out of the spaceship, making trips back and forth with armfuls of what I can only describe as "stuff". There were bits of shining metal, pieces of crystal cut into strange shapes, filmy sheets decorated with patterns of metallic lines that could have been some sort of circuit board. She'd managed to detach one of the storage compartments from the living quarters and we used that as a box beside us on the heather. I added my handbag to the collection to keep it out of the way. Princess used the duffel bag to carry more and more of these strange components from the ship and add them to the growing collection in the box beside us. It was clear that she hadn't a clue what most of them were, but was simply following Nuke's instructions. We could pick up their exchanges via the earpieces when she went into the ship. Nuke and the prisoner were apparently working on the deconstruction inside and rigging the thing up to blow.

We didn't have to wait four hours to be found. Princess was on another trip out from the ship when we saw movement along the distant road. A swarm of black vehicles was making their way in convoy. They were still a long way off, but I didn't need to see them close up to know what they were.

They were the black vans of Grey's Tower.

Over the earpiece chatter, I picked up another sound, a roaring of engines that I'd heard before. Overhead a silvery-grey craft was approaching. It was some mutant hybrid of a plane and helicopter, with rotors on the wings to hold it aloft. It strongly resembled the drone we'd used in our spying. There was no doubt in my mind that it came from Grey's Tower.

We had the high ground, a bit of cover and the alien weapons so we could probably hold our own against the troops in the vans, but the aircraft was another matter. I felt horrendously exposed as it came up overhead. We had nothing with which to shield ourselves. I felt a chill run through me as I wondered how much protection the armour would give against whatever weaponry that thing might be fitted with.

A part of me wanted to run, to get away from this army before they reached us, but there was no escape. That craft could follow me across the moors and pick me off from there.

There was no choice but to remain and fight.

Chapter 16

The craft roared overhead, hovering over the wrecked ship, but we had a little time before the vans could get to us, picking their way across rough and boggy ground. I kept my eyes fixed on the silvery machine as it hung in the air. My weapon was in hand, in case soldiers appeared from the guts of the craft. A bright spotlight set the rain sparkling and roved the ground, picking out targets. I was blinded for a moment when it fell on me, then it darted to the others, pausing on each in turn, even the unconscious body of Damian.

There was no way to hide. Despite my armour, I felt chillingly exposed.

No sign of weapons yet from the craft above us but the vans crept ever closer, the noise of their engines mingling with the roar from the air. Princess and the alien prisoner hurried from the ship, carrying the last of the stolen equipment in the duffel bag. They dumped it by the box beside Damian. Ethan and I had moved apart a little along the ridge, not wanting to be too easy a target.

I thought of the people in those vans. I wondered if I'd met them. If I'd fought beside them. If I'd talked to them at the coffee machine in the security office. Those weren't faceless mooks down there. They were people. People who probably thought they were doing the right thing.

"If we're going to fight," I said, "it should be non-lethal. We fight until we can get away."

There was a moment of silence from my earpiece. I felt like my heart stopped beating in that instant and the moment seemed to drag. What if the others decided that the only way out was through killing?

It was Knight who spoke first, probably only a couple of seconds after my statement. "Agreed."

It took a moment longer for Nuke to agree. "We knock them out. Or we steal a vehicle and disable the others. No blood spilled today."

The vans were getting closer now, six of them, dark shapes cutting their muddy way through the grass and heather. There was little enough time for strategy. Nuke was still inside the ship, working on destroying the alien tech inside. He had us fan out around the ship, along the higher ground. Each of us lay in the heather on the top of the ridge as the vans made their way up to the ship. We'd be pretty sheltered from below, but the aircraft's light kept picking us out one after the other so everyone would know where to aim.

Nuke had the big rifle now. The rest of us had our handguns. I rested on my elbows as I peered through my meagre cover, my gun ready in my hand. My fingers were tight around the handle to stop them from trembling. I couldn't block out the aircraft roar, aware of it even as I watched the approaching vans. I was bathed in light again, the rain sparkling in the air around me. In my mind, I could imagine the hatch in the side of the craft opening and a sniper leaning down to shoot me in the back.

I was lying close to the unconscious Damian, a part of me wondering if we should just hand him over to them. I knew first-hand that Grey's Tower had excellent medical facilities. But I didn't want even him to go through the suspicion that I'd had to endure.

A couple of the trailing vans were struggling through the mud that the earlier vehicles had left, but the leading one was nearly at the ship.

Nuke was there in the escape hatch, firing upwards.

A line of light cut through the air. It caught one of the whirling rotors causing a scream of metal. A jagged lump of something the size of my head smashed down into the heather just in front of me. A few more rained down, chunks of the rotor crashing down. One struck the hood of the leading van, which swerved and stopped in a screech of brakes.

I was vaguely aware of the shift in noise. The aircraft engines were louder, struggling, as it tried to gain altitude, to manoeuvre away from the fire on the ground.

I was more focused on the hunk of broken metal that was within arm's reach, its edges jagged and almost melted from the rifle's fire. If that had fallen less than half a metre nearer, it would have smashed into the back of my head. And that had been the handiwork of my supposed ally.

Nuke fired the rifle again, towards the vans this time. The ground exploded in front of the first van in a hail of mud and a sudden burst of steam. Mud rained down on the windscreen and it tried to reverse away. Its tires spun uselessly as its attempts to manoeuvre just dug itself deeper into the ground. It was about a hundred metres from the ship. As Nuke fired again, the other vans came to a stop behind the first.

I could only imagine what was going through the heads of those in the vans. They must have been wondering how many they were up against and how well armed, if there were any more of us hiding inside the ship. I was doing a quick calculation of what we might be facing. There were, at most, ten people in each van, so we could be facing as many as sixty people. Probably a mixture of glue guns and conventional weapons. The conventional weapons didn't worry me too much, but the glue guns could be a major problem. At least we had better weapons, or so I thought.

Then Nuke's voice came into my earpiece.

"The rifle's out of power. It will probably take a while to recharge."

A little piece of hope withered and died. So, now we were down to the handguns. Four Guardians, a prisoner and the unconscious Damian against maybe sixty men plus the aircraft, and now we'd lost our most powerful weapon.

A few of the van doors were opening at the back, but whoever was getting out kept the vans between us and them so it was difficult to make out anything clearly.

"Can't get a clear shot," Princess complained.

"As soon as anyone gets a shot, take it," Nuke said.

The people in the vans must have been coordinating, with each other and with the aircraft. The craft was still struggling overhead, engines straining. Those in the vans started moving all at once, surging across the open ground to the nearer of the ship's two compartments. We all fired. The air was filled with bursts of energy from around the ridge and a hail of bullets from those below.

Something dropped down from the aircraft, hitting the earth close to me. I rolled aside as it blew, a burst of fire and a shower of metal shards. I felt the shrapnel glance against the Omega armour, some striking with bruising force, along with splatters of dirt and singed heather.

Then I was on my back in the heather, beside the crater of the explosion, with the craft's searchlight focusing in on me, no doubt for a second attempt.

In that instant of terror, I remembered the first time I'd seen Nuke, a figure in the darkness aiming upwards. I raised my small handgun and fired in the direction of the light.

The searchlight died in an explosion of glass.

"Omega! Omega, are you hurt?" Knight's voice was yelling in my ear.

"I'm OK," I managed.

I risked a glance back towards the vans. A large number of men were unconscious on the damp ground, but others had reached the cover offered by the edge of the crashed ship.

Another grenade exploded near the top of the ridge. It was further away that time, but in the aftermath of the blast my earpiece was filled with furious swearing.

"Princess?!" Nuke demanded.

"It caught my leg. I'll be fine."

The armour offered a lot of protection, but it wasn't impervious. Whoever was up in that aircraft could just keep dropping grenades on us until they got lucky. In the meantime, the forces on the ground were firing towards us again. At least we had some cover from those below; the bullets embedded themselves in muddy ground without coming close to me. Nuke, though, had to duck back inside the escape hatch to shield himself.

Then I spotted a dark figure among the soldiers.

"Victory's armour!"

Someone else had been given the armour that I'd once used, stolen from one of Nuke's team. Our weapons were useless against it, energy deflected harmlessly across the surface. He, or maybe she – it was impossible to tell behind the armour – didn't bother with the cover of the ship which at least a dozen of the others had reached. He'd realised that his armour protected him and, a large glue gun in his hands, was running across the open ground to the ship's hatch where Nuke was hiding.

Nuke fired a blast from his handgun into the ground beside the fake-Victory. Fake-Victory dodged the flying earth, stumbling slightly but still running. Again and again Nuke fired, each time a deliberate miss that cut the ground to shreds but didn't touch the guy.

A few of the others were poking around from the edge of the ship compartment, firing in our direction. I fired a few shots of my own, mostly to keep them in cover and out of the way. Bullets weren't doing them much good and the glue gun didn't have great range. Right now, our big problem was the person in armour with the glue gun. I remembered the fight in the Tower and how the aliens' weapons had taken down Nuke and Princess in that same armour. But Nuke had used up the rifle's power.

There was just one other hope.

"Nuke!" I said. "Keep firing but aim at him! Keep hitting him!"

"The armour deflects the energy," Princess said.

"Not all of it."

I was thinking of our prisoner and how he'd kept firing at me until I'd felt the effects even with protective clothing. Nuke shifted his aim and fired his gun straight at the fake-Victory. From the shift in the light, he'd upped the power.

Fake-Victory ran a few more steps straight into that line of light. Then he stumbled.

I had the first inklings of a plan.

"Knight, keep those guys by the ship occupied," I said. "Nuke, keep shooting if fake-Victory comes for you again. Princess, you're the sacrifice. Break cover and try to get that guy to use up all the glue in his gun."

"Why me?" Princess complained.

"Because Nuke still needs to blow the ship and you're closer than Knight."

They followed my instructions with no further arguments. Nuke was sheltered behind the edge of the hatch firing towards fake-Victory, who was struggling to stand and trying to get a better position. Princess left her cover on top of the ridge, firing down at fake-Victory. Fake-Victory fired back, but his first shot was a little wide. Princess dodged and barely got grazed by the glue, which was setting harmlessly over the hard portion covering her upper arm.

His second shot caught her cleanly.

I left my own cover now and ran in a low crouch along the top of the ridge. Those by the ship clearly noticed me. Ringing gunshots began again.

Something struck my side and I nearly fell. Even with the armour's protection, the impact of the bullet hurt like someone had just whacked me in the side with a hammer. I managed to keep running, no doubt with adrenaline dulling the sudden pain. I tried to keep away from the ridge's edge to present less of a target.

As I started down the slope, another grenade struck behind me. The explosion knocked me forward and I tumbled from the ridge in a tangle of limbs, face-planting in the heather with left arm twisted awkwardly under me. My gun was somewhere above me.

Princess had performed her task well and was a solid mass of glue and armour among the heather. She was perfectly unharmed inside that mess, managing a disgruntled "This had better be worth it."

I turned to reclaim my weapon. I was completely out in the open now. Another bullet struck, catching me in the left shoulder. A burst of pain ran down the entire limb and I stumbled.

I was aware of light from the ridge as Knight fired towards the soldiers, keeping them busy. Ever my protector.

I grabbed my gun, holstering it just as another grenade nearly knocked me flying in a fountain of fire and shrapnel. Then I found my feet and raced down the remaining slope towards the fake-Victory. He aimed the glue gun at me but nothing came out. He'd used it all up on Princess.

I charged at him, ignoring weapons. He was trying to scramble backwards along the ground, dragging an injured leg. The armour had buckled around his right shin, maybe from Nuke's repeated fire, maybe he'd been caught when the grenade blew. I didn't really have to fight. I just got on top of him, sitting across his chest and trapping one arm with my leg. His lack of resistance surprised me. No trained fighter would let himself be pinned so easily.

He was wriggling beneath me, trying to pull free, but I could simply reach down and undo the clasp of his helmet. I pulled it off, despite the man's struggles. Then I looked down on a face I knew all too well.

Matt.

They'd put the skinny computer geek in Victory's armour despite the fact he had no combat training at all. And now he was looking up at in me in terror, as though he might wet himself at any moment. I hesitated. It hurt almost worse than the bullet impacts that someone I'd been considering a friend could look at me with such fear in his eyes.

Chapter 17

"I really hope you know what you're doing," Princess's voice muttered in my ear.

I spoke quietly, "Nuke, order them to lay down their weapons."

Those sheltering behind the ship's compartment didn't have a hope of hearing me, but Matt heard all too well. I saw terror turn to confusion and recognition.

"Jenny?" he asked.

"Ssh. Trust me."

From his point of cover, Nuke yelled, "Lay down your guns!"

I got a double dose of it, his yell coming in much too loud over the earpiece. I climbed off Matt and got to my feet, hauling him up with me. I took my gun from my holster again and aimed at Matt's head. I glanced at the side, a paranoid check of the power settings.

"Let him go!"

I knew that voice. Someone stepped away from the spaceship, throwing his gun off into the heather, hands up in a gesture of surrender. It was Thomas. His face held the same fear that Matt's had.

"And the rest!" Nuke yelled. "If you don't want your friend to die, surrender!"

I was aware that so many men must be targeting me now. Then there was the aircraft, still roaring away above. They couldn't drop a grenade on me without risking hitting Matt, but I didn't know what else they might have at their disposal. I didn't know if they'd really care if Matt became collateral damage.

I held my terror in check, glad no one could see my face, and tried to project the aura of a ruthless killer as I kept my weapon aimed above Matt's ear.

At Nuke's direction, the men tossed aside their weapons and knelt in a little group on the slope of ground, well within Nuke's line of sight. There might have been more hiding in the shelter of the spaceship and I could see that most of the vans still had their drivers. A few more yells from Nuke and the drivers got out and joined the others. About a dozen men knelt on the ground. The rest were lying in the mud, already unconscious. These guys couldn't know for sure if they were alive or dead and it seemed none of them wanted to risk it.

Thomas called out to Matt, asking if he was alright. The terrified tremor in Matt's voice was genuine.

"Just do as they say!" Matt begged.

We sent Knight down to check the Grey's Tower men, to make sure no one was trying to be a hero. Then he had the job of getting Princess down the slope and into the van. She was muttering complaints in my ear about being manhandled as Ethan stuck her into the furthest vehicle. I just stood there, an arm holding Matt up and the other holding the gun to his head.

"How long have you worked for them?" Matt asked.

"Since Professor Swinson warned me not to trust Mrs Grey," I answered, "and was murdered for it. Mrs Grey is the bad guy here."

I don't know if he believed me. I kept talking anyway, hoping that some of it would sink in.

"I don't want us to be enemies," I said quietly. "You're a good guy, Matt. Don't trust Mrs Grey. Figure out what the Tower is really about."

By then Knight had got Princess stowed and returned for the unconscious Damian. Nuke sent our prisoner over to help him, but I was too busy watching the Grey's Tower men to see them do it. Knight made one more trip to get the box of "stuff". I waited, tensely worried that someone would decide to stop us. My eyes flicked from man to man, watching for any movement, any sign that one might be going for another weapon.

If Matt tried to run, or warned them it was a bluff, then we were dead. The hand holding the gun threatened to start shaking again.

Nuke had ducked inside the ship. He emerged now, hurrying across the open ground towards the van. I was backing towards the van as well, half-carrying Matt. His leg was clearly not taking his weight, but he was doing what he could with his other leg to help me. The eyes of the Tower men were watching us every step of the way.

We passed them.

"Look up!" Knight's warning came a second too late.

Darkness enveloped me from above.

Something large and dark fell on me, shrouding me in confusion and blindness for a moment. I let go of Matt, fighting to free myself from what covered me. It was a camouflage tarp, dropped from the aircraft.

As I shook it off, pain erupted in my chest again and again. The force knocked me backwards, all breath gone. I fought for air against the bursts of agony in my stomach and ribs. Thomas was closing the distance between us, firing from a small handgun. It clicked, empty of bullets, as I gasped on the ground.

Knight fired from behind me. Thomas crumpled.

Matt lurched over to him, a yell of distress on his lips.

The other Tower men were on their feet, weapons reclaimed, ready to fire in our direction. I could barely move thanks to the burning torment of my chest. I didn't know how much more I could take.

The ship erupted in white and blue fire. It started in the far compartment but flashed along the rest of it, a torrent of flames pouring through the escape hatch. The whole thing blazed in bright, hot fury, the whole skin of it somehow burning. All I could think was that it shouldn't have been possible. If the ship could burn like that, it wouldn't have made it through the atmosphere.

The Tower men hit the ground as heat and fire raged above them. The craft wheeled overhead, engines straining.

I could barely see for the brightness of it all.

Someone was behind me, grabbing me, Knight's voice in my ear telling me to get up, insisting that we moved. His hands were hauling at me. I think I must have got my feet moving, but it's difficult to remember it. All I could see was the burning ship, branded on my vision.

Knight dumped me into the back of the van and then raced round to the front.

"They left the keys in the ignition," Knight panted.

The van roared to life.

The aircraft moved overhead as our vehicle turned. In the light of the burning ship, I saw the hatch on the side of the craft, a gaping hole with perhaps more terrors within.

A gun fired. The energy line tore from the open door of the van, catching the undamaged rotor. The craft seemed to lurch sideways, engines struggling, fighting against gravity and losing. It was only a few hundred metres above the ridge, dropping altitude with ungainly shudders.

The van rocked along the rough ground and I got a clear view through the open van door as the aircraft made an undignified landing behind the ridge. Our supposed prisoner was standing in the open door of the van, clinging desperately to a handle with one hand and aiming Princess's gun with the other. He was the one who'd fired the shot and killed the aircraft.

He'd probably just saved our lives.

Now he dropped the gun and grabbed for the door handle, slamming it shut. He collapsed onto the floor of the van, terror and shock obvious on even an alien face.

One of the Tower guys must have found a gun because bullets tore through the metal doors of the van. I crouched low, bending myself over Damian to shield him until we left the Tower men and the gunfire behind us.

***

There was a bottle of the glue solvent in the back of the van, so Nuke and I were able to unstick Princess. As we got her free, she started to remove pieces of armour. She looked across at me.

"You owe me," she said.

"I got us out of there alive," I said.

She considered, "Fair enough. We're even then." She thought. "Actually, we came to rescue you."

"And got the teleporter blown up in the process," I protested. "You don't get points for that. Knight does, but you don't."

It was strange, cheerfully bickering about what might, or might not, count in terms of debts. I think we were just relieved to be alive.

I needed both Princess and Nuke to help me remove my armour. My movements were stiff and painful. Most of my torso was protesting against even the slightest shift. My left arm didn't want to cooperate, pain throbbing along the length of it. I'm not ashamed to say I cried. When even breathing hurts, it's hard to do anything else.

With Navy coordinating everything from the base, we rendezvoused with Bats and Valiant, who'd come for us in a white van with a rental company logo on the side. It was a simple matter to transfer the stolen technology from one van to the other. Damian was less simple, but he regained consciousness as Knight and Nuke were trying to figure out how to carry him across.

I just worried about getting myself across. My legs were about the only part of me not injured, but even so, walking that short distance was a problem. Still, I climbed up into the van and sat myself on the floor of it, watching Valiant tending Damian's injuries with a fairly basic-looking first aid kit.

"You do not look like a doctor," Damian said.

"I'm studying nursing," Valiant answered.

"What are you? Twelve?"

"Seventeen. Now shut up or you don't get painkillers."

Chapter 18

It took us several hours to get back to base. I still wasn't sure where it was exactly, but the fact it was clearly a long drive south of York at least explained why our searches north had been unsuccessful. It was dark by the time we got there. I felt exhausted, starving, pained and thoroughly drained. Valiant checked me over and declared that I didn't have any broken ribs, though the bruising and swelling would probably hurt for several days. I swallowed a painkiller and sat back to feel every jolt of the van sending new waves of pain through me.

Bats and Knight were taking turns with the driving so I still hadn't had a chance for a real conversation with Ethan.

They pulled the van into the car park of a dingy business centre. There were lots of buildings of tired brick, made duller by the dark sky and ever-present drizzle. A few had cars or vans parked outside them, but most of the parking places were empty. The one we'd parked in front of had a garage door-style roller that lifted up, allowing us access to the inside. The inside was just as I remembered from my brief visits here, with long tables and a mishmash of electronics of indeterminate purpose.

Damian walked inside, his torso swathed in gauze from Valiant's ministrations in the van. He looked around at dirt and duct tape. Navy came over to greet us, obviously delighted to have us returned safe and sound. He wasn't in armour but in torn jeans and a T-shirt bearing an equation joke. Damian looked appraisingly at him too, apparently with no better opinion.

"How did we ever think you guys were a threat?" he asked.

"We're the ones with the prescription-strength painkillers," Valiant said. "Maybe you should stop with the insults."

"At least he's not calling you sweetheart every five minutes," I commented.

It was a weird evening. Though that word loses some meaning after spending most of the day on a spaceship. Navy prepared us some food in a tiny kitchen area off the back of the main room. It was just pasta and cheese, at which Nuke made some comments about the lack of vegetables, but he joined in with us anyway. I was starving at that point and would have eaten just about anything.

There was a little camp bed set up in a small office area off the back of the main warehouse, where Knight had apparently been living recently. We gave that to Damian who, despite Valiant's threats, was dosed up on painkillers and very groggy.

Our prisoner was a bit of a problem. Bats went out and came back shortly with a Rosetta Stone program for learning English. We stuck the prisoner in front of a computer with that running and let him get on with it. It seemed Nuke wasn't all that worried about him running off or doing anything he shouldn't with the equipment lying around the base. I really wish I knew what had happened between the two of them on the ship, but he had just helped us to escape, so I guess that earned him some measure of trust.

I spent a long time filling the others in on every detail of what I'd seen and heard on the ship. We went over it several times until I was as bad tempered as Damian. It was Knight who suggested that maybe I'd had enough.

At that, Knight and I retreated to a back corner of the warehouse where we could talk with some degree of privacy. I was thoroughly worn out, so I just sat down on the floor, leaning against the wall. Knight slid down to sit beside me, a careful distance between us.

"I've missed you," he said.

"Yeah. I've missed you too."

"When we got the emergency signal and the teleport failed, I was really worried. I thought maybe... Maybe something had gone wrong."

"Something did go wrong."

"I mean…"

"You thought I'd died?"

"Jenny… Omega, everything has been so messed up for us recently, but it hit me hard when I thought you were in trouble. I just…" he trailed off again. He leant his head back against the wall with a faint thump, "God! I'm really bad at this stuff."

Across the room, despite the pretence that they were otherwise occupied, at least one of the team had clearly been watching us and seeing Knight struggle.

"He wants to start dating again," Princess yelled.

Knight started laughing.

"What she said."

I laughed too at the absurdity of trying to be romantic in such a bizarre situation. Or maybe it was the euphoria that my Knight was still interested.

"I'd like that," I said. "After all the mess and secrets, let's just start over. Clean slate."

He grinned and offered me his hand.

"Sure," he said. "Hi. I'm Ethan, also known as Knight."

I returned the grin and placed my hand in his, "Jenny, codename Omega, pleased to meet you."

And we laughed at our private moment in this very unprivate place.

***

I wish I could say that the story ended there, so at least this chapter could have a happy ending. We were all alive and safe. We had the files that Navy and Nuke were decoding, believing them to be descriptions of some of the research taking place in the Tower's labs. We'd acquired items from the alien ship that Navy was excitedly investigating, using some of them to fix the fried teleporter. We'd even gained two new members of the team, however reluctantly they might have volunteered. And Ethan and I were starting afresh, rekindling our relationship.

But there was one more disaster to occur just as we were starting to enjoy this breathing space. A few days after the crash, I was getting rid of my work phone when I saw a final message on it. It was from Thomas, asking me to meet him urgently. We were concerned it might be a trap, but Navy had got the teleporter up and running again and I had a new emergency signal. So, we found Thomas's address, a neat semi-detached on the outskirts of York, at the good end of Tang Hall Lane. Navy teleported me into the back garden. I left my armour behind and my gun. It was just me.

I knocked on the back door. Thomas opened it with a surprised look on his face, then grabbed me and pulled me inside, taking a furtive look around in case anyone had seen me. I followed him through a little kitchen and into a small living room, where he hastily closed the curtains. He stood in front of me, shifting nervously.

"What's going on?" I asked.

"You're Omega?" he asked back.

I nodded, "Matt told you?"

"He told me what you said to him during the ambush."

"Is he here somewhere?" I asked. "If we're going to talk, probably best to tell you both at once."

There was a long silence. I looked at Thomas, seeing the frantic worry in his shifting posture.

"What's going on?" I asked again.

Thomas went over to a dresser that stood against one wall. He opened a drawer and pulled out a piece of paper with writing printed on one side. He handed it to me and let me read. It was a "Dear John" letter. Matt said that he was leaving and was sorry and that he had to do this by letter because he couldn't bear to do it face to face.

"He was looking into the situation at work," Thomas said. "He wanted to find out if you'd been telling the truth, so he was accessing the computers. Then Lucy called him out for a meeting and he didn't come back. I waited and finally checked the logs and they said he'd already left the office. When I got home, I found that. Some of his clothes were gone, his laptop and stuff like that."

"He left you?"

"That's what it's meant to look like, but he wouldn't do this. Even if we were to split up, he wouldn't just walk out. And he left stuff he'd never leave. I called his mum and she hasn't heard from him. The police won't take me seriously. They think I'm just in denial about being dumped, but I know that something's happened to Matt. He must have found something in the computer systems, something that incriminates the Tower. And they made him disappear."

He looked close to tears. Before now, I'd seen Thomas as a strong athlete, a fighter, or a cheerful soul stealing food from Matt's plate in the canteen and laughing about it. Now I saw him broken and I wished I could offer meaningful help. I reached out and laid a hand on his arm.

"We'll figure this out," I said.

"How?"

I knew right then what I had to ask of him and I knew first-hand how difficult it would be.

"You have to go back into Grey's Tower," I said. "They know for sure now that I'm working for Nuke, but they don't know what Matt told you. Go back in. Do what I couldn't and figure out what Mrs Grey is planning. When we know more, we can figure out what happened to Matt."

Thomas nodded.

"If they've hurt Matt," he said, "I'm going to kill them."

"It'll be OK. We'll find him."

I almost believed it. I was persuading my friend to go back into the place I'd fled, to find the secrets that had been hidden from us. I knew all the dangers and I knew the difficulties, but still I was telling Thomas to take my place as the traitor in the Tower. And he agreed, because I'd said that we could find Matt and he'd be OK.

God, I was a fool.

About the Author

Jessica Meats has a passion for both writing and technology. She got a degree in Mathematics and Computer Science from the University of York, where she was a founding member of a creative arts magazine. She now works in the technology industry and uses that experience to fuel her stories.